LITTLE DARK DEEDS

GEORGIANA GERMAINE

CHERYL BRADSHAW

LITTLE DARK DEEDS

Georgiana Germaine Series, #12

By *New York Times & USA Today*
Bestselling Author

CHERYL BRADSHAW

"How miserably things seem to be arranged in this world. If we have no friends, we have no pleasure; and if we have them, we are sure to lose them, and be doubly pained by the loss."

Abraham Lincoln

1

Tiffany Wheeler rushed around the walk-in closet, yanking clothes off hangers and stuffing them into her suitcase. One quick glance at the clock on the bedroom wall, and she sighed. She was running behind. If she was going to make it to the airport in time to catch her flight to New York City, she had to be out the door in the next forty-five minutes, and she hadn't even showered yet.

Grabbing her terry-cloth bathrobe off the end of the bed, Tiffany headed for the bathroom, turning the shower's handle as she stepped inside. The cool water splashed onto her back, and she winced, wishing she'd allowed the water temperature to heat up first. But today, time was not on her side.

Tiffany reached for the soap, her thoughts turning to tomorrow and the wedding of one of her closest friends, Georgiana Germaine. Tiffany had known Georgiana since elementary school, though they'd had a rocky start. One day in the school cafeteria, Tiffany noticed a bag of chips inside Georgiana's A-Team lunchbox, and she snatched it, thinking no one had seen the dirty deed. But two boys at the opposite end of the table had, and when Georgiana accused them of thievery, they were quick to point fingers, singling out the offender.

As Tiffany tried making a run for it, Georgiana sprinted in her direction, hands fisted. She punched Tiffany square in the nose, breaking it. Blood sprayed all over Tiffany's pastel-pink dress, and it wasn't long before every eye in the room was on them. From then on, many of her fellow classmates called her Squirt, and Georgiana became her sworn enemy.

Years passed before Tiffany and Georgiana spoke again, when one day Georgiana found Tiffany hiding under the bleachers, mourning the traumatic breakup with her boyfriend. She'd indulged in a bit too much tequila, which had been supplied by a friend, and was far from sober. Knowing Tiffany was in no condition to go home, Georgiana decided to call Tiffany's mother and pretend she needed help on a school project. The plan worked, and for the next several hours, Tiffany rested in Georgiana's bedroom, chugging water until she was sober enough to head home.

Ever since, the duo had been the best of friends.

Thinking back on it now, Tiffany laughed. Life could be crazy, but at times it had a way of mending hearts—hers and Georgiana's, at least. As happy as Tiffany was for Georgiana's upcoming nuptials, Tiffany's own love life was in shambles. A week ago, when Tiffany was in her law office, a woman rushed through the door and burst into tears the moment they made eye contact. The woman's name was Jana, and she'd come to deliver a terrible truth. Tyler, the man Tiffany had been dating for over six months, was married—*to Jana.*

Tiffany had spent the past several days grieving the breakup, her heart in pieces. The man she thought was different than the rest—a man she hoped to marry one day—had been fooling her all along, and she'd fallen for it.

Again.

It wasn't an ideal time for her to be attending a wedding.

But tomorrow wasn't about her.

It was about Georgiana.

And she was determined to push her feelings of discomfort to the side and put on a happy face for her dear friend.

Returning to the present moment, Tiffany reached for the shampoo. Popping the lid open, she squirted a dollop onto her palm, then rubbed her hands together to create a thick lather. She worked it into her long, blond hair, and as the suds fell over her face, she heard what sounded like a door closing. Through the muffled sound of the water, she couldn't be sure.

She rinsed the suds out of her eyes, moved the shower curtain to the side, and peeked out, listening.

A breeze drifted by. She guessed it was from the window she'd left open in the bedroom. It had been a windy day—perhaps the wind had blown something over.

Deciding it was nothing, Tiffany shrugged, dipping beneath the water for one last rinse. She shut the water off and stepped out, bending down to reach for her bathrobe, which had fallen on the floor. She wrapped it around herself and turned, panic flooding her mind as she came to the realization she was not alone.

An intruder stood in the bathroom's doorway, knife in hand.

With no way to escape, she stepped back. "What are you doing here, in *my* house?"

There was no response.

Fearing the worst, she said, "No, please. Don't hurt me."

Her pleas for mercy fell on deaf ears, the knife lifting and then plunging down—again, and again.

As Tiffany drew her last breaths, one thought ran through her mind—if Georgiana would have been in her position, what would she have done?

2

Twenty-nine years after I first laid eyes on Giovanni Luciana on a sunny, clear college day had brought us to this moment—our wedding day. When we first met, I was a young, impressionable college student who'd just turned eighteen. And while we became close friends during those years, when I learned he'd become engaged to Valentina Violeta Romana, I was gutted, like the light within my soul had been snuffed out.

I realized something that day: I didn't just *like* Giovanni, I loved him.

But our courtship would have to wait.

Many years later, after Giovanni had married Valentina, his sister, Daniela, admitted he didn't love his wife, not in the way she deserved, and the feeling was mutual. The marriage hadn't been a match between two people in love. It had been an arrangement made by their fathers, a way to bring two powerful families together. And though Giovanni had protested the marriage, in the end, he still went through with it.

Nonetheless, I went on to marry Liam, a man I loved, though it had always felt like something was missing between us. Never a believer in the notion of soul mates, or finding my "one true love," marrying Liam seemed right at the time, until it wasn't.

Decades later, after Liam and I divorced, I found myself reminiscing one night about my college years and how precious time was, how fleeting. Up to that point, I hadn't lived my best life, not by a long shot. A familiar face came to mind, and I wondered where Giovanni was, what he was doing, and if he ever thought of me.

As my curiosity grew, I located a book he'd given me all those years ago, *Sense and Sensibility*. Inside, he'd inscribed a message, and below it, a phone number. I figured the number had changed after all these years but decided to take a leap of faith, a decision that would change our lives forever.

It turned out he was single, and when I admitted the same, he invited me to join him for dinner at his New York City restaurant, Osteria dei Mascalzoni, or "Tavern of the Scoundrels."

It was there our love story began.

Now, almost five years later, love felt a lot different in middle age than it had in my younger years. The young, naïve Georgiana who hadn't believed in soul mates was far more pliant and open-minded. After all, I'd found mine.

I was sitting in front of the mirror, admiring my spaghetti-strap, floor-length, ivory-colored bridal gown. With its thousands of hand-beaded pieces, it looked like something straight out of a Gatsby novel. The bias-cut sheath design had been cut on a diagonal, a stylistic technique causing the fabric to drape, creating a slinky silhouette. It was the most gorgeous gown I'd ever worn, and I couldn't wait for him to see it.

Down the hallway I heard brisk footsteps moving in my direction, followed by, "Yoo-hoo, pardon me. Mother of the bride coming through."

She burst into the room, her curly, bob-style hair bouncing

as she scampered my way. She looked me up and down and lifted a finger, swishing it left to right, head shaking. "For goodness' sake, dear. Let's get a move on. We've less than ten minutes before it's time to walk down the aisle. Your shoes aren't on, your hair ... well, is in desperate need of a touchup, and your makeup needs a bit of attention too."

I turned, glancing in the mirror, unsure of what all the fuss was about.

She clapped her hands together. "Come on. Hop to it!"

I reached out, taking her hand in mine. "Breathe, Mom. We'll make it on time. Don't worry."

"Don't *worry*? All I ever do is worry. It's a mother's job."

She waved me off and turned, shuffling back to the hallway and calling for Tiffany, my childhood friend.

Hands on hips, my mother muttered a frustrated, "Where on earth is she? She was supposed to be here ages ago to help you get ready. What kind of friend leaves someone on red on their wedding day?"

I tried to stifle a laugh and failed. "*Leaves someone on red?*"

"It's what all the cool kids say nowadays."

"Are you sure about that?"

"Of course. Your niece says it all the time."

My niece was only twelve, which felt a little young for her to be fluent in modern slang.

"When I see Tiffany, I'm going to give her a piece of my mind," my mother huffed.

"Maybe she's running late."

I'd said the words, knowing it wasn't like Tiffany to be late —ever.

And given I'd been so caught up in memories of the past, I hadn't been paying close attention to the time. If I had, I would have realized she was over an hour late.

"I'll try her cell phone," I said.

"There's no time. You have a mere six minutes before the ceremony begins. Time to whip things into high gear."

I sighed and slipped on my two-inch heels. Facing the mirror, I adjusted the white-and-gold iridescent leaf and floral headpiece pinned to the side of my head. Then I reached for my lipstick, a lovely neutral shade that added a tinge of color without becoming a focal point.

Certain the final touches I'd added were enough, I looked at my mother for approval. Based on her expression, I wasn't sure I'd get it.

"What now?" I asked. "Today is supposed to be a calm, joyful day. You're stressing me out."

"Oh, dear. I'm sorry. I just want everything to be perfect. You deserve it. You deserve it all."

"Everything *is* perfect."

Aunt Laura poked her head into the room, smiling as she looked at me. "Are you two about ready?"

"As ready as we're ever going to be," my mother replied.

I stood, and my aunt pressed a hand to her lips, saying, "You're the most beautiful bride I've ever seen. Your father would have been so proud."

At the mention of his name, tears formed in my mother's eyes. "Taken too soon. I always thought he would be the one walking you to the altar. It surprised me when you didn't ask Harvey."

I threw my arms around my mother. "I love Harvey. I couldn't ask for a better stepfather. But as soon as Giovanni proposed, I knew it was you I wanted by my side today."

She leaned back, swishing a hand through the air. "As much as I cherish these rare sentimental moments of yours, not another word, darling, or all three of us will end up with streaks of makeup all over our faces."

I nodded and looped my arm around hers.

She lifted a finger, declaring, "Now, let's get you married!"

3

It was just about time for me to step through the doorway leading to the sweeping gardens of the Luciana family estate, where friends and family were waiting for the upcoming nuptials to begin. My niece, Lark, was standing a few feet in front of me in a puffy, taupe dress, her long, blond locks swept into a loose braid that dangled over her shoulder. In her hand was a basket of white rose petals. And ever since she arrived, she'd been counting down the hours until it was time for her to scatter them.

Lark looked over at my sister, Phoebe, eyes beaming as she said, "Mommy, is it my turn yet?"

Phoebe nodded, and Lark turned toward me, smiling as she reached into the basket and descended the stairs leading to the back of the estate.

Then it was Luka's turn.

Attaching a ring inside a velvet box of my Samoyed's collar that morning had been met with a fair amount of resistance, but in the end, he allowed it. Leash in hand, my aunt coaxed him out the door.

Moments later, the crowd went quiet.

The sound of rustling was heard, followed by a trumpet bellowing out the first few bars of Louis Armstrong's "La Vie en Rose," a song Giovanni and I had chosen for this magical moment. Translated, the song's title meant "life in pink," to aspire to see the beauty in each day together.

My mother leaned in close, kissing me on the cheek.

"Are you ready, dear?" she asked.

"I am."

We made our way to the lawn, and I paused, taking in the smiling faces of all those who'd gathered for our special day. We strolled by aisle after aisle, and as we neared the area the ceremony was to take place, my focus shifted from the guests to *him* —the one man who'd always made everything seem right. With him, I felt safe, and loved, and seen. And most of all free. Free to become the woman I wanted to be, despite my shortcomings.

As I looked into his eyes, a tear rolled down his cheek. He didn't acknowledge it, made no attempt to wipe it away. His attention was fixed on me and me alone.

My mother gave him a wink, slipping her arm out of mine as I took my place in front of him. He stood a moment, then took my hands in his, leaning toward me as he whispered, "You're an absolute vision, my darling."

I felt the heat rising in my cheeks, and I smiled, squeezing his hands as we turned toward the officiant, Silas Crowe, a man who'd been a close friend and confidant of mine for many years. Most days, he dressed like a laidback, surfer in board shorts, T-shirt, flip-flops, and his trademark messy, sun-bleached hair. Today, he looked like a different man in crisp, coffee-colored linen pants and a cream-colored button-up shirt, his untamed hair twisted into a tight, sleek bun.

Silas looked at both of us and said, "Are you two ready to get your wedding on?"

We nodded, and he turned his attention toward our guests.

"Welcome friends, family, and loved ones," he said. "Please be seated."

I scanned the audience, taking in the smiles on every face, and felt a wave of love drifting through the warm summer air.

"Thank you for taking the time to gather on this charming summer evening to share in this special day with Georgiana and Giovanni," Silas said. "I've known Georgiana for several years now, ever since she was hired as a police officer for San Luis Obispo County in California. We've been lucky enough to work together on many cases over the years, Georgiana as a detective, and me as the county coroner. What started off as two associates working together to bring cases to a close, has now turned into a lifelong friendship."

He paused, thumbing at Giovanni, adding, "I'll never forget the first time Georgiana told me about the new man in her life. I recall thinking to myself, 'Who is this guy,' and 'Why was she so cryptic when I ask about his family?'"

Silas laughed as did many in the crowd, but a few of the older gentlemen on Giovanni's side of the family crossed their arms, eyes narrowing at Silas like they questioned what he would say next.

I wasn't worried.

Silas had a talent for bringing people together.

Today would be no exception.

"I'll admit I've always been protective of Georgiana, wanting nothing but the best for her," Silas said. "About a year after they started dating, Giovanni bought a house in Cambria, and he suggested they move in together. I remember asking her if she loved him. She didn't hesitate before telling me she did, and then she said something that shocked me. She admitted she'd loved him for years, ever since their college days."

A piercing whistle rang out from the crowd, followed by

clapping and cheers. Giovanni said nothing but tipped his head toward our feisty, rambunctious crowd.

Silas grinned, waiting for the audience to calm before he continued.

"As I was saying, the more I listened to Georgiana talk about Giovanni that day, the more confident I was that Giovanni wasn't just some man from her past. He was the man of her future. It's been my privilege to get to know him, a man I consider among the most trustworthy, stand-up people I've ever met. And Georgiana, or 'Gigi' as I often call you, I'm going to tell you and everyone else something most of you don't know, something Giovanni gave me permission to say today."

I braced myself, anticipating what was to come.

"Right before you and Giovanni moved in together, I stopped by one day so we could have ourselves a little chat," Silas said.

"You did not," I said.

"I sure did, and I wasn't alone." He raised a finger, pointing out a few attendees in the front row. "Your mother was there, as was your stepdad, Harvey, and your Aunt Laura."

My mother began shaking her head, her face flushed and tense, as if panicked she'd been outed. Harvey smiled, and as for Aunt Laura? She slapped a hand to her knee, belting out a hearty laugh, unfazed.

"Go on, then ... tell us what happened," Giovanni's sister said.

"I'm sure you can all guess why the four of us decided to speak to Giovanni that day," Silas said. "We wanted to get a better feel for the man who had fallen for the woman we care so deeply about. We entered Giovanni's home not knowing what to expect. And when we left, we looked at each other, and we were all of one accord. I stand before you today, speaking from the heart, and I can say with certainty—we all knew that day that Giovanni and Georgiana were meant to be together."

More clapping and cheering followed.

When it quieted down, Silas began our vows, starting with the usual, "Do you take Georgiana to be your lawfully wedded wife ..."

Giovanni agreed.

I did the same.

Silas moved through the rest of the traditional vows with one exception. At my behest, he left out the "'til death do us part" part. I never wanted to part, not in life, and not in death. If I had my way, when the day came for us to leave this earthly life, I hoped we'd find ourselves on another plane, or another time, or in another existence. If there was a way back to each other, we'd find it.

The ceremony concluded with Silas saying, "And now, as we celebrate this amazing relationship, the couple has each written vows they'd like to share. Giovanni, why don't we start with you?"

Giovanni glanced at me, clearing his throat as he took in a deep breath in. "Georgiana, I remember the first time I laid eyes on you. You were sitting beneath the grandest tree at school, dressed in a gingham skirt and a black cardigan. You were barefoot and running your toes through the grass. Your dark hair was pulled into a loose bun, and you were reading a book, paying no heed to the world going on around you. I stood there staring at you for some time. I had no idea why I was so taken aback by you. All I knew was ... I was besotted. I decided then to find out who you were, and once I did, I made some changes to my college schedule. The fact we ended up having a few classes together may have seemed like a coincidence, but it was not. One day, I overheard you telling a classmate that you were looking for a roommate. I stepped in and put you in touch with my sister. The two of you moved in together, and our friendship began. It wasn't long before I started feeling something more. I wanted to tell you. And now, thinking back on it, I ... I ... I should have ..."

His voice cracked as he struggled to find the words he wanted to say.

He cleared his throat, then continued.

"Five years ago, when you reached out to me, I was given a rare second chance to make something more of my life. The chance to do what I should have done the first time around. And though we hadn't seen each other in many, many years, being in your presence again, it was like no time had passed, and we picked up right where we left off. Our love story began, and today we turn the page on our new chapter, the chapter of our future. You are everything to me, *cara mia*, and it is my privilege to be by your side, a place I promise to remain forever."

He closed his eyes, shedding a few tears, and I reached out, brushing them away.

Silas gave the moment the time it deserved, and then said, "Beautiful words from a beautiful man. And now, Georgiana, I'll turn it over to you."

In my lifetime, I'd been known to speak my mind. But public speaking in front of an eager crowd, ready to cling to my every word wasn't my forte. The same could be said for sharing sentimental feelings. But I saw today as an opportunity, a chance to push myself out of my discomfort to pay respect to the man I loved.

Our eyes met again, and I began. "Giovanni, I remember the first time I knew I loved you. We'd decided to play hooky one day, and the two of us drove to Coney Island. I couldn't believe I'd been living in the area all that time and never thought to go there before. We were walking on the beach, talking about our families, and you looked over at me and smiled. You didn't say a word, but it was obvious there was something on your mind. As we finished our walk, you mumbled something under your breath, something you may have thought I didn't hear, even though I had. You said you'd always wondered whether there could have been something more between us. It was something I felt like I'd been waiting for you to say, and I spent the next few days trying to sort out my feelings. There was so much I wanted to say to you. I pictured myself grabbing your face, blurting out my love for you. But in the end, life had another plan for you at that time, and I couldn't bring myself to do it. I moved on, and you moved on, and hey … it was only a short twenty-four years before I said to myself, 'Maybe it's about time I tell the guy how I feel.'"

A wave of laughter rolled through the crowd, laughter I was hoping for when I'd decided to include that part. It was the perfect interlude, lightening the mood just enough without taking away from the sentimentality of the moment.

Daniela cupped a hand to the side of her mouth, shouting, "Well? Did you tell him?"

I shot her a wink. "We're getting married today, aren't we?"

"Good for you!"

It was good for me, and so was he.

Turning back toward Giovanni, I said, "At this stage in my life, I'd reconciled myself to the fact that true love, the kick-you-in-the-gut kind of love, wasn't going to happen for me. And then there was you and me and a perfect dinner date, a night that changed our lives forever. Because of you, I've learned how to be vulnerable again. Because of you, I've learned to trust. Because of you, I'm no longer content going through life on my own. You've made me a better person, a happier person, the person I'm always striving to be. I love you, Giovanni, and I want nothing more than to be your wife."

As my declaration of love came to an end, many wedding

attendees were overcome with emotion. The sentiment meant everything to me, knowing the message I'd waited so long to deliver had resonated in the way I'd intended.

Rings were exchanged, and then Silas wrapped it up. "As I stand before you today, officiating this heartfelt ceremony between two people destined to be together, reunited in the love they have for one another, I'm proud to declare Giovanni and Georgiana husband and wife! Let us stand, showing our support to a couple we know and love. Giovanni, it's time for you to kiss your bride."

Everyone shot out of their seats, clapping, whistling, and cheering, and Giovanni swooped an arm around my back, dipping me back as he went in for a kiss. Then he took my hand, and we walked together between the aisles.

Looking around, we nodded, thanking guests for their well wishes as we passed. A moment later, I found myself distracted, scanning the crowd for the familiar face of a friend—a friend who was nowhere in sight.

4

"What is it, darling?" Giovanni asked.

I crossed one leg over the other, trying to avoid souring our wedding day by expressing my concerns. But he knew me too well, and he knew when something was off.

"Tiffany was supposed to be here to help me get ready for the wedding," I said. "She never showed. After the ceremony ended, I looked through the crowd, and I didn't see her. I don't think she's here."

"Is it possible she missed her flight?"

"I think she would have texted me to let me know if something happened. I checked my phone before the reception. She hasn't called or texted."

"Why don't you give her a call?"

"It's our wedding reception. Everyone wants to talk to us, dance with us, celebrate the night. I don't feel right about ducking out to track Tiffany down."

"I'm not suggesting you track her down tonight. You said you had one more dress change before the DJ starts his set in half an hour's time. Go, get changed, and give Tiffany a call."

Wanting to remain present on my special day, I hadn't carried my cell phone around with me. Today was about us and our guests, and in the spirit of savoring every moment, I'd left my phone behind in our room.

The urge to check in with Tiffany was too tempting, and I stood.

"I'll just be a few minutes," I said. "I'll be back before you know it."

"Take all the time you need. I'll inform the DJ not to start without you."

We kissed, and I smoothed down the front of my second dress of the evening, an ivory, one-shoulder crepe dress with a feathered cape sleeve. A black, sequined floral pattern ran across the top and down one side, tapering off at the waist. The dress was just about knee length. And where the fabric ended, two feet of fringe began, running all the way down to my three-inch, strappy heels that sparkled whenever they hit the light.

I grabbed my vintage pearl-beaded clutch off the chair, slipping the chain-link strap over my shoulder as I searched for the easiest way out of the reception tent. No one was at the back of it, and I decided exiting that way was my best bet if I wanted to avoid any interactions. I headed in that direction. It worked in my favor until I stepped outside and found Harvey on the phone, pacing back and forth, his expression one of distress. We made eye contact, and his eyes widened as if he was surprised to see me.

He lifted a finger, indicating I should wait a moment, and then turned back to the call, saying, "I'm sorry, I need to go. I'll let him know."

He shoved his phone in his pocket and looked at me, saying nothing. There was no mistaking the emotion in his eyes—emotion I felt wasn't associated with my wedding.

"Harvey, is everything all right?" I asked.

He cleared his throat once, then twice. "Of course, why wouldn't it be?"

"I know that look. You're worried about something, aren't you? What's happened?"

"I ... ahh, I was just thinking about how wonderful your ceremony was, and I got a little overwhelmed, that's all."

It wasn't all, though.

He was keeping something from me, deflecting.

"I came outside to get a bit of air," he added. "What about you?"

Whatever was troubling him, he didn't want to discuss it. Not right then, at least. Maybe it was personal in nature. My instincts told me not to press the matter, but given we'd always been close, it was just what I wanted to do.

"I'm headed to my room," I said. "I need to change before the dancing starts."

"You have a *third* dress?"

"I sure do. I figure I'm never getting married again. May as well make the most of it."

He shrugged. "Makes sense, I suppose."

"I'll auction off everything I've worn today and donate the proceeds to charity."

Harvey walked toward me, embracing me in a hug. "I'm so proud of you, of everything you've done with your life ... of the woman you are today, and the woman you've always been."

"And I'm grateful for you. I am that woman because of your guidance."

He made a sweeping motion with his hand. "Oh, I don't know about that. I was just trying to step into your father's shoes. Big shoes to fill, to be sure. You run along and get changed now. I better get back in there before your mother comes looking for me."

I nodded, knowing she'd materialize at any moment.

Harvey ducked back inside the tent, and I entered the house, which was teeming with staff hired to oversee the reception. Food was coming in and going out, along with trays of champagne and dirty dishes being replaced with clean ones, as they prepared to transition from the reception dinner to the fun stuff —the dessert. And by dessert, I mean charcuterie boards, and a wedding cake made of layers of stacked cheese wheels. There'd be sweets for those who wanted a sugary treat, of course, but as for me and my house, we would eat cheese.

I left the buzz of the main hall, ascending a long flight of stairs before arriving in the biggest of the guest suites, which came complete with its own living room, two full bathrooms—one for each of us—and a bar area.

I kicked off my shoes, flexing my toes as I gave my feet a much-needed rest. Then I took great care in removing my dress, slipping it off and placing it back on the hanger inside the plastic bag it came in. I hung it in the closet and reached for the bag containing my third and final dress of the night. Unzipping it, I took a moment to admire the white, above-knee party gown. Its flapper, fringe-sheathed design with tiny white beads and feather hemline had caught my eye months earlier when I saw it in a vintage clothing shop. The moment I saw it, I knew it was the perfect dress to end a perfect night.

I laid the dress out on the bed and moved a hand to my hips, looking around.

"Now where did I set my phone down ..."

I found it on top of a pillow and reached for it. There were several calls and even more texts, none of which were from Tiffany. I scrolled through my contacts until I found her number. The call went through, and the phone rang and rang. I hung up and tried again. This time, it went straight to voicemail.

My first thought was to be snarky, to let her know how I felt about her being a no-show. But without knowing what had happened, that approach didn't feel right. She wouldn't stand me up. It wasn't like her.

I settled on:

"Hey, Tiffany. I missed you today. *We* missed you. It was a perfect day. Well, perfect except for you not being here. I'm not sure why you didn't show up or why you're not here now, but all I care about is that I hear from you. I'm not sure if you missed your flight or if something else came up, but I'm starting to get worried. Call me, please, as soon as you get this message. I need to know you're all right."

I ended the call and walked to the bathroom, taking a few moments to touch up my makeup before pulling my wavy, plum-colored, shoulder-length locks back into a sleek bun at the nape of my neck. As I slipped on my dress, my phone buzzed. Hoping it was Tiffany, I raced across the room to answer it and was met with disappointment—a text from my mother.

Hurry back down, dear. The DJ says she won't start playing her set until you arrive. Your guests are getting restless. Toodaloo!

I had no doubt our guests were fine. The booze had been flowing for over three hours now. They weren't restless. They were soaking in the sauce, eager to get their dance on.

Slipping my shoes back on, I felt immediate pain, my feet begging to be free after all the hours I'd spent in heels. I debated my options and then slipped them back off, dangling them between a few fingers as I went barefoot, maybe even for the rest of the night.

Besides, this bride didn't need to follow the rules.

Not when she was so dang good at breaking them.

5

It was a little after three o'clock in the morning, and I was in bed, cozying up to Giovanni whose arms were wrapped around me. He brought my hand to his lips and said, "I hope the wedding was everything you'd hoped it would be."

"It was one of the best days of my life."

I could think of only one happier time in my life, the day I'd given birth to my daughter, Fallon. Her life had ended too soon, and while she was never far from my thoughts, today she felt especially near, like she was with me in spirit, alongside my father.

"I thought I'd be asleep by now, but I'm still a little wound up from the day we had," I said.

"Me too."

"I'm glad we changed our honeymoon plans. Holding off for a couple of weeks will give us time to relax before our European vacation."

"Speaking of Italy, what are you most excited to see while we're there?"

"The Sassi in Matera."

Matera, a place steeped in history, had stood for over nine

thousand years, making it one of the oldest inhabited cities in the world. The enchanting area was most known for the Sassi, ancient cave dwellings carved into limestone cliffs. Often referred to as "the second Bethlehem," its history dated back to the Paleolithic era. I'd spent years dreaming of visiting this place, and now, at long last, that dream was soon to become a reality.

"Matera is a place like no other I've been before," Giovanni said. "I believe you'll enjoy Florence just as much. Several years ago, I considered purchasing a villa there. It's one of the few places you can immerse yourself in another culture, another way of life."

"Why haven't you mentioned the idea of buying a villa there before?"

"It's not something I see in our present. In the distant future, perhaps. I prefer to be close by, here for you."

I gave him a playful poke to the chest. "What makes you think I'd be here and not in Italy with you?"

"Your career, for one."

"I won't always be a detective. I imagine one day I'll retire, sell the business, or leave it to someone I trust to keep it going."

He let out a slight laugh. "I can't imagine you'll retire any time soon."

"*Soon*, no. But one day."

"All the more reason to wait. If we bought a villa in Italy, I'd want you there by my side."

I hoisted myself up on my arm, leaning in for a kiss. "I'd want to be by your side too."

As I pondered what life abroad might be like—long days spent strolling along the charming, locally owned café's, gelato in hand—he jolted me out of the thought with a question.

"Not to put a damper on the end of our day, but have you heard from Tiffany?"

"I haven't. I considered calling her father, Ron, but by the time it crossed my mind, it was much too late. I'll try her again when we're up for the day. If she doesn't answer, I'll give him a call."

I'd known Ron Wheeler since elementary school. He'd been one of my teachers. He wasn't too fond of me at first, given the rivalry Tiffany and I once had. By the time I graduated, and our friendship was going strong, he softened toward me. Years later, he became mayor, and I a police officer and then a detective. During those years, we worked together on some of my more public cases, though since he'd retired, we hadn't seen each other much.

As Giovanni drifted off to sleep beside me, my eyelids grew heavy, and a smile crossed my lips.

Today I had a new name: Georgiana Germaine-Luciana.

It had a nice ring to it.

6

My eyes flickered open, and I found myself in the home Tiffany had purchased in Cambria back in 2021. It was an older home, and during its remodel, she'd discovered something shocking—a body hidden within the walls. As I sought out the identity of her mysterious John Doe, the investigation took an unexpected turn. It turned out John Doe's death was tied to the murder of my father, who'd died in a hit-and-run accident when I was a child.

It was then I realized my father's death was no accident.

One murder to be solved became two.

And solve them, I did.

In the past few years, our schedules had been busy, and Tiffany and I hadn't spent as much time together. A couple months earlier, we met up for lunch and promised to make a bigger effort to see each other once I was married.

At present, I was sitting in Tiffany's living room, wondering why I was there when she didn't seem to be, and not being able to recall how I got there in the first place. I was dressed in the same white satin brocade nightgown I'd worn to bed, which confused me even more.

What was I doing here?

And why?

It felt a lot more comforting to remain in denial, to believe everything was fine … that Tiffany was safe, happy, and alive. To believe she had a good reason for skipping our wedding. Every fiber of my being wanted to believe it, even though not one fiber did.

If she was fine, I wouldn't be here.

I stood, shouting, "Tiffany, are you here?"

I was met with silence.

Given my familiarity with the house, I began nosing around. Tiffany's suitcase was next to the front door, all packed up and ready to go. Her purse rested on top. I rummaged through it, finding her cell phone. There were several missed calls. Not just from me, but from a handful of other people, including a call from my mother.

Setting the phone back inside her purse, I shifted my focus to the master bedroom.

The bed was made, but there was no sign of her. It was then I noticed the bathroom door was closed. I walked toward it, reaching for the knob.

"You shouldn't go in there."

I gasped, whipping around to find Tiffany sitting on the bed in a bathrobe, even though she hadn't been there moments before.

"Is this what it's like?" she asked.

"I don't understand the question."

"Your dreams. Is this what they're like, the ones you've always told me about?"

"We don't know that this dream is one of *those* dreams. I went to bed with you on my mind. Makes sense I'd dream about you."

It was a half-truth, and I expected she knew it.

"Of course, it is, Georgiana," she said. "You may not want to accept what's right in front of you, but you have to, sooner than later."

"If it's one of those dreams it would mean that you're ..."

"Dead. It's all right. You can say it."

"I won't. It can't be true."

She slapped a hand against her knee. "Not true, eh? Tell that to the jerk who murdered me."

I sat down beside her, a wave of nausea twisting my gut. "Can we talk about it, about what happened to you?"

"Where's the fun in that?"

I pulled a pillow over my lap and leaned against the headboard. "I knew something was wrong when you didn't show up for the wedding."

"How was it, by the way?"

"We shouldn't be talking about my wedding. We should be talking about you."

"Why? The topic of your wedding is so much more interesting. And hey, sorry I didn't make it, but you know ... I got delayed."

Permanently, it seemed.

I pointed at the bathroom door. "Is that where it happened?"

She nodded. "Not the classiest way to go out, is it? I was stabbed. Didn't feel too good, either. Death by stabby-stab. Yeah, I don't recommend it."

Even in death she'd managed to maintain her quick-witted sense of humor.

"I can't imagine why anyone would want to murder you," I said. "Ever since we were kids, you were always the one everyone liked."

"Well, people have their reasons."

"Speaking of which, what happened?"

"There you go again, shifting the conversation back to murder."

"I can't help it."

I glanced across the room at a series of framed photos on the dresser, homing in on one in particular. Two girls, arm in arm, posing in caps and gowns, beaming with pride as they held up their high school diplomas.

So young, so innocent.

So much life ahead of them.

But one of those had just been cut short.

"I'm not ready to accept what's happened," I said. "I'm going to wake up in the morning and give you a call, and you're going to answer. You're going to tell me you didn't make it to the wedding because your flight got canceled, or delayed, or you missed it because you got held up in traffic. Anything, as long as it's not ..."

The truth.

Tiffany hopped up, moving a hand to her hip. "Do you want to see your wedding gift?"

"Sure."

"Stay here. I'll be right back."

She left the room, returning with a wrapped gift.

Setting it down in front of me, she said, "Go on, open it."

I stared at it for a time, my emotions cresting as reality set in.

The tears came, and I let them.

Attempting to lighten the mood, she said, "Has anyone ever told you that you have a horrible cry face? I mean, one of the worst I've ever seen. You look like a depressed basset hound."

"A depressed basset hound? Even if their faces are sad at times, they're still cute, right?"

"They are. Not you, though."

I wiped my eyes, even though the tears showed no signs of stopping.

"I know just what you need to cheer you up," Tiffany said. "I'll be right back."

This time, she returned with a bag of chips, the same kind she'd stolen from me in grade school.

She tossed the bag at me, erupting with laughter. "It was my wedding gag gift. I couldn't help myself. Brings back memories, doesn't it?"

"Yeah, memories of you nicking them from my lunch bag."

"Who knew you'd get so irate over a stupid bag of chips."

"You learned what happens when you come between a girl and her favorite snack."

Even though I felt lousy, I managed to crack a smile.

"That's better," she said. "Open your present, and don't be all dainty and stuff with the paper. I don't have all day. Or do I? Who knows? I'm new at this 'entering your dreams' stuff."

I grabbed the wrapped gift, tearing the side open as I removed the bubble wrapped contents inside. Getting past the ridiculous amount of tape she'd used took some time, but it was worth it. The gift was a large, round piece of wood. Etched in the center was a tree with the initials G & G inside a heart.

"I love it," I said.

"I knew you would. I remembered your love story ... and you saying the first time Giovanni saw you was when you were sitting under a tree on the college campus. And he proposed to you in the exact same spot. Figured you could find a place for it in your house."

"I will, and I'll always think of you when I look at it." I set the gift to the side. "Can we talk about you now?"

Tiffany sat on the edge of the bed, her expression sullen. "If we must."

"Does anyone know you're dead?"

"Yeah, word's starting to get around."

"When were you found?"

"I don't know. Since it's the middle of the night, yesterday, I guess."

"Who found you?"

She hung her head. "My ... uhh, my dad. He was supposed to be giving me a ride to the airport."

I thought about the conversation I'd had with Harvey the night before, about how solemn he'd been. Had he known then what I was learning now? Had everyone? Had they all been keeping it from me?

"I'm sorry," I said.

"I don't think I'll be here much longer."

"What do you mean?"

"I don't know. It's hard to describe."

"Try," I said.

"It's like my spirit body is being pulled away from here, away from this place."

"Is there anything you can do to stop it?"

"I wouldn't even know how to try. What happens to the those you've communicated with in other dreams?"

"Every person is different. The most common thing that happens is they'll be talking to me one minute, and the next, they start to fade away until they're just not there anymore."

"Then I'd better say what I've come to say."

"Go on."

She nodded, taking a breath. "Will you do something for me?"

"Anything, name it."

"Will you look out for my dad? Will you help him through what's happened? I don't want him to go through life not *living* it. He's always lived for me, you know? My happiness is his happiness. He lives alone. I'm worried."

"I'll be there for him. You needn't worry."

"Good, then I've said everything I need to say."

"Wait, what do you mean?"

"I can't help it, Gigi. It's time for me to go. I can feel it."

"Please, not yet. We haven't even talked about your murder."

She swished a hand through the air. "You don't need me. You can figure it out on your own. Lean into your intuition, and hey, thanks for ... well, always having my back. You were a great friend. I wish we had more time together."

I opened my mouth, planning to return the sentiment then stopped when she started to fade, a little at first, and then a little more, and then I was alone, as if I had been alone the entire time.

My friend was gone, and she wasn't coming back.

Not today or any other day.

7

I shot up in bed and gasped. Looking around, I didn't see Giovanni. A moment later, he rounded the corner with a cup of tea in his hand. He gave me a curious look and said, "What's wrong?"

Without thinking, I blurted, "I think Tiffany's dead."

He set the cup of tea on my nightstand and sat beside me. "How can you be certain?"

"I dreamed about her."

"And you're sure it was one of *those* dreams?"

"I am."

"It would explain why she didn't make it to the wedding. Tell me about your dream."

"She was stabbed in the bathroom. It happened yesterday when she was getting ready to head to the airport. And do you want to know what bugs me the most? I think a handful of people at our wedding knew about it."

He pressed a hand to his chest. "I can assure you, I know nothing. It may have been our wedding day, but something as important as this, I wouldn't have kept it from you."

"I know."

"We need to get to the truth."

"I know just the man to talk to—Harvey."

"Why him?"

"I saw him last night when I left the tent. He was on the phone with someone. When he saw me, he ended the call. We chatted for a minute, and he was acting strange." I stood, wrapping a robe around me. "I'm going to see if he's in his room. I'll be right back."

Darting into the hallway, I made a beeline for the suite Harvey and my mother were staying in. I knocked once, and my mother opened the door, blinking at me but saying nothing, which wasn't like her.

"Where's Harvey?" I asked.

"Well, good morning to you too, dear."

She fell silent once more, lingering in the doorway without extending an invitation for me to enter the suite.

"I need to talk to Harvey," I said. "Is he here?"

"What do you need to talk to him about?"

We stared at each other for a moment, the expression on her face telling me what her words did not.

"How long have you known?" I asked.

"About what?"

"Be straight with me, please. I know you know about Tiffany."

She placed her hands on her hips. "Now, Georgiana, listen to me."

"I mean no disrespect, Mom, but I am all out of patience right now."

I heard what sounded like a sliding door opening and then Harvey walked toward us, sighing as he said, "It's fine. We knew this was coming. Putting it off won't change anything. What's done can't be undone."

My mother threw her hands in the air. "Oh, all right, come

in. We can talk outside on the balcony."

As I followed them to the back of the suite, my mother began mumbling.

"I just don't understand what's wrong with people. You give a person one simple task. *One* task, to keep quiet. And they can't even manage it."

"If you're thinking someone told me about Tiffany, they didn't," I said.

In truth, someone *had* told me.

That someone just wasn't among the living.

"If no one told you, how do you know?" my mother asked.

"Let's just say it was a gut feeling. Yesterday, when she didn't arrive for the wedding, I knew something was wrong. If something had come up, she would have told me."

"I'm sorry it happened this way, on the day of your wedding, no less. We've been worried sick about when the right time would be to give you the news. We didn't want to spoil your special day, but we should have known you'd figure it out on your own. I'm guessing you've also noticed a few of the overnight guests have gone."

"Your room was my first stop. By guests, I assume you mean Foley, Whitlock, and Silas."

"They left as soon as the reception was over, hopped on a red-eye flight."

It made sense.

Rex Foley was the chief of police in San Luis Obispo County. He was also married to my sister. Whitlock worked under him as a detective.

The three of us took a seat at the bistro table outside, and Harvey began cracking his knuckles. It was one of his tells, something he always did when he was nervous. I'd noticed him doing it last night. I just hadn't thought much of it until now.

Before we had a chance to get to the details, there was a knock at the door.

My mother threw her hands in the air. "My goodness. What now?"

"Come on in," Harvey shouted. "Door's open."

I craned my neck, curious about the unexpected visitor, relieved to see it was Giovanni.

He walked over, setting the tea I'd left in our room in front of me. "I apologize if I interrupted your conversation."

I pulled out and looked at him. "Why don't you join us?"

He nodded and sat down.

I looked at Harvey, then my mother. "What do you know about Tiffany?"

"Well, what had happened was, we were sitting at a table at the reception watching everyone enjoy the evening," my mother said. "We started chatting about what a wonderful day it had been and how it couldn't have gone better. Then Harvey received a call from Tiffany's father, Ron, who delivered the awful news. Harvey talked to Foley and Whitlock, who'd just heard about what happened themselves. The four of us debated whether we should tell you, and we decided the news could wait until today."

"I hope you know we were just trying to look after you," Harvey added. "If we'd told you last night, we knew what you'd do."

He wasn't wrong.

My first thought this morning was just how fast I could pack and get to the airport.

"You understand our predicament, don't you?" my mother said.

"I do," I said. "I can't say I'm happy about it, but I do."

"I suppose you'll want to run along home now, though it's a shame to get all wrapped up in an investigation so soon after your marriage. You should be spending time with each other, enjoying these first days together."

Giovanni reached over, grabbing my hand. "We have the rest of our lives to do that."

We did.

The same couldn't be said for Tiffany.

I turned toward Harvey. "What can you tell me about her murder?"

Harvey scratched his head. "Tiffany's father was the first to find her. He arrived at her house, texted her that he was there, and he didn't get a response. He honked the horn. Still nothing. Then he got out of the car and tried the front door. It was locked, but he knew where she kept a spare key. He used it to open the door, and ... I'm just so sorry to be the one to have to tell you this, Georgiana."

"No matter how hard it is for me to accept, it's better for me to have all the details."

He nodded and continued. "Ron found Tiffany on the bathroom floor. She'd been stabbed multiple times. He checked for a pulse, just in case, even though he didn't think there'd be one, and then he called for an ambulance. I heard from Foley and Whitlock about an hour ago. They're at her house now."

"What did they say?"

"From their initial search, they found nothing missing or taken. There was an open window in her room, which the killer may have come through. Her purse was with her luggage by the front door. There was a couple hundred dollars in cash in the wallet."

Meaning, it wasn't a robbery.

"I just don't understand why anyone would murder such a sweet woman," my mother said. "Can you?"

"She'd been seeing a new guy," I said. "I've never met him, but she seemed happy with how the relationship was going so far. I think she said his name is Tyler. I'm not saying he had anything to do with her murder, but who knows?"

"I suppose you'll be heading home now."

"I will be, yes."

"I expect we'll do the same," Harvey said. "In the meantime, is there anything we can do for you?"

"We'll speak to Giovanni's sister and let her know what's happened. In the meantime, if you see any of our remaining guests, please tell them we had an emergency back home and give them our apologies."

"Will do."

Giovanni stood, pushed his chair in, and I did the same. Then we said our goodbyes. With a new plan in motion, Giovanni went to find his sister, and I made my way back to the room, mind racing and anger simmering. I'd find the person responsible for the little dark deed of Tiffany's death, and when I did, I had half a mind to do to them what they did to her.

A life for a life.

Seemed like the perfect justice to me.

8

It was a somber flight home, but with Giovanni at my side, I managed to get through it. We didn't speak much, and we didn't need to—just being together and sharing the same space was all the support I needed right now.

We landed at a small airport a few miles out of town, and once we were off the plane and through the lobby, I saw Whitlock standing outside his vehicle, waiting. He greeted me with a nod and walked over, shaking hands with Giovanni and then wrapping his arms around me.

"How are you holding up, kiddo?" he asked.

"I don't know," I said. "I'm numb, I guess. It doesn't feel real. It's hard for me to accept that she's dead."

"I get it, and I'm sorry. Hey, ahh ... Harvey called me after you left Giovanni's family estate. He told me you two were on your way home, and I wanted to be here to greet you when you arrived. Figured you'd have a lot of questions."

"I do, but our driver is here to pick us up," I said.

"It's not a problem," Giovanni said. "I can send him home and stay with you, or if you prefer, I can head home and leave the two of you to talk."

I considered my options.

"I'd like to talk to Whitlock and Foley, and I want to go to Tiffany's house," I said. "Why don't you go home, and I'll touch base with you later?"

Giovanni nodded and leaned in, kissing me on the forehead. "If you need me for anything, call, and I'll be right there."

We said our goodbyes, and I climbed into the passenger seat of Whitlock's SUV.

"What would you like to do first?" Whitlock asked. "Would you like to talk for a spell? Or would you like to talk while we drive, do a little multitasking along the way?"

"Let's talk on our way to Tiffany's house."

"You got it."

He started the vehicle and pulled out, turning down the music so it wouldn't get in the way of our conversation.

"Has Silas been to Tiffany's house yet?" I asked.

"Uh-huh. Silas, Foley, and I went straight over as soon as we returned to town. When I left to come here, he was processing the scene with his new assistant, Kiera. Bet they'll still be there when we arrive."

"It's surreal, you know, to catch up with a friend not knowing you're never going to see her again," I said, reflecting. "Life has a way of throwing curve balls, things we don't see coming. All we can do is find a path through it, a way to keep on going, even when it's hard."

"Isn't that the truth. Hey, since you and Tiffany were so close, I've been meaning to ask ... can you think of anyone who had a motive to kill her?"

I shook my head. "She was happy the last time I saw her. Everything in her life seemed to be going great. And I can't think of anyone who would want to kill her."

"Tell me about that visit, if you don't mind."

"We hadn't seen each other for a while, so we spent a lot of time catching up."

"What did you talk about?"

I gave the question some thought. "Most of our conversation was just an average conversation between two women. But she did tell me she was seeing a new guy."

"You get a name?"

"I want to say it was Tyler. I've seen her giddy about men in the past, but with this guy, it was different."

"In what way?"

"She said even though they hadn't dated long, she thought he was her soulmate, her forever person. And the thing is, she didn't believe in that type of thing before he came along. I asked her what it was about him that made her think he was the one."

"And what did she say?"

"She thought she connected to him on a deeper level than she had with the men in her past. I guess they first met on a Sunday, so their song was *A Sunday Kind of Love*."

"Etta James. Good stuff."

"Great stuff. Tyler was a lot more attentive than other guys she'd dated. He gave her flowers every week, and then one day, they were out shopping, and she spotted an emerald necklace she liked. The next day, he bought it for her."

Whitlock raised a finger. "Could be attentive or could be too good to be true. Sounds like the man was laying it on thick. A little *too* thick, perhaps?"

"I had the same thought, though I never verbalized it. I didn't want to poke holes in her blissful happiness. And besides, given I'm living my own blissful life with Giovanni, guys like that are still out there."

"I should say, yes. I'd like to think I'm a bit of a gentleman myself."

"From what I hear, you're an exceptional gentleman. How

are things going with my aunt, by the way? I saw you together at the wedding, looking cozy, I might add."

He tapped a thumb to the steering wheel. "Laura is a funny bird, the kind that's hard to keep once you catch it, though I keep trying."

"Is everything all right between the two of you?"

"I should say, yes. She's a wonderful woman. It's just ... I'm not getting any younger. I turn seventy-two next month, and you know something—if there was one thing I'd like to have, it would be the two of us living together."

"I'm guessing you've talked to her about it."

"A few times. And look, I get that she doesn't want to get married and that she thinks living together won't allow her the independence she needs, but I think it would be splendid."

"I know how much she cares about you. Who knows? Maybe she'll come around."

"I'm not too sure. She's set in her ways, as feisty as they come."

"So was I ... and look where I am now, married to a man I never thought I'd ever see again after college. Hey ... speaking of marriage, Tiffany was supposed to bring the new guy to the wedding. Not long before she died, she texted me and said something came up, and she'd be coming on her own."

Whitlock raised a brow. "Did she explain the *something* that came up?"

"She didn't. I texted her back and asked how things were going with the guy. She said she'd tell me all about it after the wedding, which didn't seem like a big deal to me at the time, but now ..."

"You're thinking something may have happened between the two of them."

"It's possible. I'm sure I'll be able to track him down. I just need his last name."

Whitlock turned, smiling at me. "I just may be able to help you out."

"How so?"

"When you told me his name was Tyler just now, I remembered something. We found a day planner on the counter in the kitchen in Tiffany's house. When I opened it, I noticed a pocket in front. Inside, we found a business card for a man named Tyler Seymour. And get this, there were hearts drawn on the back of the card in red pen."

I guessed the hearts had been drawn by Tiffany. When we passed notes to each other in high school, whenever she talked about a guy she liked, she drew hearts around their name.

"What business is Tyler in?" I asked.

"Real estate."

"It makes sense. When we met up, she said she'd been looking into buying a second house as an investment rental."

"Huh, wonder why she gave you the guy's name but didn't tell you what he did for a living?"

"Tiffany's been through some rough breakups over the years. Whenever she was seeing a new guy, she gave me a little information at the start. She'd wait a few months because she didn't want to 'jinx it.' She did say she expected their relationship would move fast, and as long as they were still going strong by the time my wedding came around, she'd tell me everything I wanted to know about him."

We pulled up to the house, and Whitlock parked curbside, right behind Silas' VW bus.

Turning toward me, he said, "Listen, kiddo, I know you're a tough cookie. A much tougher cookie than me. But this is one of your closest friends. Seeing the crime scene of such a good friend ... well, I just want to make sure you're ready for it."

When it came to family, friends, and loved ones, was anyone ever *ready for it*?

"I appreciate your concern," I said. "And I know you're trying to look out for me. But if I'm going to investigate her murder, I need to see everything *and* know everything, whether I want to or not."

He went quiet for a moment, then said, "There is another option, you know. Not that you'd agree to it."

He didn't even need to tell me what the option was; I knew what he was getting at.

"Is the other option to step away from it and allow you and Foley to investigate without me?" I asked.

"It is our job to find out what happened and give her the justice she deserves. If it's too hard, it doesn't have to be yours. This isn't like your other cases. It's personal. I may not be the detective you are, but I'm not too shabby. And I wouldn't let up until we caught the guy, or gal, responsible."

"You're a great detective. And I've worked personal cases before. Yes, they're hard, and they take a lot out of me, but they're far more rewarding when they're solved. The way I see it, the more of us looking into her murder, the better."

"I figured you'd say as much. I just wanted you to know that you have our full support. Promise me one thing, though. If it ever feels like too much, I need you to tell me."

It was already too much, and I was in more pain over her death than I thought possible. And I hadn't even stepped foot inside her house yet.

9

The first thing I noticed upon entering Tiffany's house was her luggage leaning against the wall next to the door, purse sitting on top, as if she was still there, ready to jet off to my wedding. Beside those items was a wrapped gift. The paper was different than the one I'd seen in my dream, a pastel pink with white stripes, but the shape of the gift was the same.

In the kitchen, I found what appeared to be a few tiny drops of blood on the rug in front of the sink. Odd, given it was on the opposite end of the house from the master bedroom. I continued through the house, and I found Silas hunched over a coffee table in the living room, dusting for prints. His head was bobbing up and down to what I assumed was music playing through his earbuds. Given the brisk pace of his head movements, and the fact he was a fan of '80s metal bands, I had a decent idea of the music he was playing.

When he failed to see me, I leaned forward, tapping him on the shoulder. The gesture caught him off guard, and he leapt back.

"Whoa, Gigi," he said. "How long you been standing there?"

"Not long. I just got here."

He removed the earbuds and shoved them into one of the pockets of his black shorts. "What a difference a day makes, eh? Yesterday I was officiating your wedding, and today ..." He paused, then added, "I'm sorry. That was insensitive, wasn't it? I shouldn't have said what I just—"

I swished a hand through the air. "It's fine. I appreciate it, but you're right. It's hard to believe all that's happened in the past twenty-four hours. My main focus is to find who did this to her. How's everything going on your end?"

"Slow, but that's on me. Knowing what she meant to you, I'm taking my time. I don't want to miss anything. I'm sure I'm being a bit *too* meticulous, but hey, if it helps us catch this dude, it will all be worth it. I could use a break, though. You wanna sit for a minute and talk?"

"Sure."

We took a seat on the sofa, the same sofa I'd helped Tiffany pick out when she'd bought and renovated the home several years earlier. We'd been goofing off in the furniture store that day, bouncing up and down as we went from sofa to sofa, looking for one that was firm, but not *too* firm.

That same day, she met Furniture Salesman Chad, who, after selling her the sofa set, asked if he could give her a call sometime. They dated for about nine months, and when they broke up, via text message no less, she didn't give me a lot of details about what happened. All she said was they had an argument—one they couldn't seem to recover from.

Thinking back on it now, it was becoming clear that Tiffany had kept me out of the loop a lot more than I'd realized. At times, she was an open book. Other times, she was elusive, and when it came to friends, I didn't like to pry. The way I saw it, if someone I cared about wanted to share information about their life with me, I gave them the time and space to do it.

When I was conducting an investigation, on the other hand, I relished the art of prying—poking and prodding a person until all the juicy details came spilling out. I saw it as a gift—an art form if you will—and I was dang good at it when it suited me.

"Hey, if you don't feel up to talking, I don't mind just sitting here with you," Silas said.

"Oh, no. We can talk ... sorry."

"Where'd you go just now?"

"I was thinking about this sofa. I was with her the day she bought it." Glancing around the room, I added, "We were together when she picked out everything in this room. Except for the wall art. The cat dressed in a ballerina costume over there was *not* my idea."

He turned toward the framed print and fisted a hand over his mouth, laughing. "I think the cat art is the most dope thing in this place."

I wasn't surprised.

"How long have you been here?" I asked.

"Four or five hours. I would have liked to have been here before Tiffany's body was removed, but Kiera did a great job of photographing the scene and gathering the initial evidence in my absence."

With his workload picking up in recent years, Silas had been given permission to hire an assistant. And that was Kiera, a charismatic, energetic young woman in her late twenties.

"So, you've seen Kiera's photos?" I asked.

"Yep. She forwarded them to me right before I boarded the flight."

"What are your initial thoughts and takeaways?"

He crossed one leg over the other, giving the question some thought. "Here's what I know so far. Tiffany was stabbed several times, and the wounds she sustained weren't isolated to one area."

"Meaning?"

"They were haphazard, like wherever the arm flailed and landed was it. Some stabbings are a lot more methodical, like a slit throat or a knife through the heart. One and done. Not this one."

"Sounds like it was more sporadic. There may be something there. A crime of passion, perhaps?"

"Or a novice who didn't know what they were doing and was taking swings and trying to land them before Tiffany had a chance to fight back."

"*Did she* fight back?"

"I'm not sure yet. From what I've seen so far, I'd say no. We took some fingernail scrapings. Once we've had the chance to run some tests, I'll have a more definitive answer for you."

"What can you tell me about the time of death?"

"Based on Kiera's review of the scene, the murder took place not long before Tiffany's father arrived to take her to the airport. He called 911, and when the paramedics got here, they reported her skin was pale, in a state of pallor mortis. Given her body temperature was close to normal at that time, she hadn't entered algor mortis yet. Bottom line, she hadn't been dead long."

The way she'd been murdered seemed rushed—not well thought out, at least.

Had it been a random act of violence?

A crime of passion?

Something else?

"It seems risky to me, murdering her right before she was planning on heading to the airport," I said. "Even if the killer had no knowledge of her trip, they would have noticed the luggage at the door ... *if* they came in that way. Given her bedroom window was open, it could have been an easier way to get inside the house. Were there any signs of forced entry?"

"The lock on the front door looks like it's had some damage to it. A bit of paint is chipped off around the knob, and I noticed some scratch and dent marks too."

"Her door was always like that," I said. "I kept bugging her to fix it."

In that moment, I realized something—something important.

"I bought Tiffany a doorbell security camera for her for Christmas last year," I said. "If the killer entered through the front, there should be footage. Have you taken a look at it?"

"It was the first thing Foley did when he arrived."

"And?"

"Turns out, it wasn't on during the time of the murder, and for who knows how long before that. The battery was dead."

I huffed out a disappointed sigh.

I'd purchased and installed the camera myself, and when I'd given it to her, I made sure to tell her how important it was for her to use it. She'd waved it off, laughing as she reminded me how little crime there was in our quaint little town.

Little crime didn't mean *no* crime.

But when it came to convincing others of that fact, it wasn't easy.

What *was* easy was for people to assume crimes of this nature were things that happened to other people, and *not* to them.

"Even though we have no footage, the fact she had a camera would have been obvious to anyone who approached her front door," I said. "I would think it would give a person pause, maybe think about another entry point so they wouldn't be seen. If it turns out the killer came through the front door, I'd assume they knew Tiffany. Maybe they even knew the camera wasn't on."

"The murderer may have also worn a mask or a disguise of some kind."

Silas was right.

I was trying to put the clues together too fast, jumping to conclusions without thinking them through first. In most of my homicide investigations, my mind was a lot clearer, but given the murder was so personal to me, I knew I wasn't thinking straight, not as much as I should be. If I was going to figure out what happened to Tiffany and why, I needed to focus, to treat her murder like I would any other.

It was a reasonable thought.

I just wasn't sure it was possible.

"Have you had the chance to look Tiffany over yet?" I asked.

"For a short time."

"Did anything other than the stab wounds suggest a motive for her murder?"

From the look on his face, he knew what I was getting at.

I just couldn't bring myself to say it.

Silas cleared his throat. "I'll be doing a forensic exam to see if she ... uhh, you know, was ..."

"Raped before or after she was murdered."

There was an uncomfortable silence, which wasn't something that happened between us all that often, and I sensed his concern for what I was going through. I imagined others would behave the same way, whether I wanted them to or not.

I was trying to be tough, to act like I could handle this investigation in the same way I'd handled all the others. But if I was being honest with myself, part of me wanted to melt to the ground, ranting and wailing until all my pent-up frustration was spent.

Tiffany had been taken from me, and it wasn't okay.

It wouldn't *ever* be okay.

But right now, I had a job to do.

And I needed to find a way to do it.

"Can you describe the crime scene to me?" I asked.

"Anything in particular?"

"Was she dressed, or was she naked? And if she *was* dressed, what was she wearing?"

"She had on a robe. Most of the robe came off during the murder, but it was still over one of her arms when she died. When Tiffany's father found her, her breasts and genitals were exposed. He admitted to covering her with a towel."

"Do you believe Tiffany was stabbed with a knife, or is it possible a different object was used?" I asked.

"A knife was found about a foot away from her body."

How odd.

"Why leave it?" I asked. "You would think the killer would conceal it somehow, taking it with them when they left."

Silas shrugged. "Why, indeed. There was a fair amount of blood on the knife's handle and on the blade."

"Any prints?"

"We didn't find any."

To me, that indicated the killer had worn gloves, suggesting premeditation.

I was about to ask a follow-up question, when I heard sniffling, and I looked up, my eyes coming to rest on the one man I wasn't prepared to face yet.

10

Ron Wheeler wiped his eyes, blowing his nose into a handkerchief as we made eye contact. The first thing I wondered was how long he'd been standing there, listening to Silas and I go over all the horrifying details of his daughter's tragic end.

I stood and approached him, pulling him in for an embrace. Then I took a step back and said, "Hey, I … I'm sorry it took me so long to get here. I just heard the news about Tiffany this morning, or I would have been here sooner."

"How was the wedding?"

"It was …"

Not right to talk about my best day when it was his worst.

"Listen, with all that's happened, we don't need to talk about it right now," I said.

"Oh, I don't know. It beats talking about the reason we're all here. Wouldn't you agree?"

His eyes were bloodshot, puffy and red, and I was certain he'd done a fair amount of mourning in the last twenty-four hours. His hair was disheveled and sticking out all over, like he'd wrapped his hands around a live wire. And his clothes were loose and wrinkled as if they'd been worn for hours on end.

I doubted he'd slept much at all.

He looked at me like he knew I was making a silent assessment of his person. As if sensing the awkwardness of the situation, Silas gave me a nod and ducked out of the room. With the two of us alone, I wasn't sure what to say or what to do. Maybe it was because there wasn't anything *to* do. No amount of consoling him would change the fact that his daughter was dead.

"Ron, I ..."

"You know what I keep thinking?" he said. "What if I had arrived earlier to pick her up for the airport? Thirty minutes, an hour, two hours. I could have saved my little girl, and none of this would have ..."

As soon as the words left his mouth, he bent over, his shaking hands pressing onto his knees as he began saying "what if, what if ..." over and over again. With each repetition, he became louder, the sounds of a broken father echoing throughout the house.

It wasn't long before Foley rounded the corner, eyes wide when he saw Ron.

He approached us, placing a hand on Ron's shoulder. "Ron, you shouldn't be here right—"

Wiping the tears from his eyes, Ron said, "Oh, come off it, Foley. This is *me* we're talking about, the former mayor of the city, may I remind you."

"I understand, it's just ... protocol."

"Screw protocol. I'm her father. I have every right to be here."

"It's just, we're still processing the scene."

"No kidding. I won't touch anything if that's what you're worried about."

"It would just be better if you—"

Ron thumbed in my direction. "Oh, so what you're saying is it's okay for Georgiana to be here, but not me? Haven't heard you ask *her* to leave yet."

Foley gave me a nervous, look like he was struggling to come up with an adequate response. He landed on, "I've asked Georgiana to assist us on this case."

It was a lie, of course.

He hadn't asked me yet, though I expected he would.

It didn't matter to me one way or the other.

He knew me well enough to know I would be conducting my own investigation, with his permission or without it.

Ron turned toward me. "That true? You working together on the investigation?"

"We are."

The way I saw it, the invitation had just been extended, and I was all too happy to accept.

"You sure you can handle it?" he pressed.

"I'm not sure of anything right now, but for Tiffany's sake, and yours, no matter how I'm feeling, I'll work through it."

He nodded, satisfied. "If there's one thing I know for certain, if anyone can figure out what happened to my daughter, it's you." He tipped his head toward Foley, adding, "No offense, but you know I'm speaking the truth. I mean, you're good. Georgiana's ... well, it's like she was born to do this work."

"No offense taken," Foley said. "Working together will make it all go a lot faster, I hope. Like you, we want answers. The sooner, the better."

Ron nodded. "That's why I'm here, to offer my help."

"The best thing you can do right now is to focus on taking care of yourself. Go home. Get some rest. We got this, Ron."

"I'm not going anywhere," he insisted. "Even if I did, it wouldn't matter. I can't eat. Can't sleep. Perhaps if I contribute to your investigation in some way, it'll help. Doubt it, but it's worth a try, isn't it?"

Foley may have wanted him to leave, but Ron was resolute.

He wasn't going anywhere, not until we gave him what he wanted.

Why not give the man just that?

"I have a question," I said.

"Now we're talking," Ron said. "Go on."

Foley shot me a warning look, which I ignored.

"I had lunch with Tiffany a few months ago, and she mentioned a new guy she was dating," I said. "She was supposed to bring him to the wedding, but then she texted me last week saying something came up, and he wouldn't make it to the wedding. Do you know why their plans changed at the last minute?"

"I ... yeah. It's one of the reasons I wanted to talk to you. She didn't want you to know what happened. She feared it might put a damper on your nuptials."

"I don't understand."

"The real estate guy she was seeing, Tyler Seymour ... he's married."

Married?

I couldn't believe it.

"The way Tiffany talked about him, she thought they had a future together," I said.

"Yeah, she had high hopes for the relationship. When she found out he was married ... well, devastated isn't even the right word to describe how she felt. For a few days, she didn't even go to work. And you know Tiffany, she was somewhat of a workaholic. She lived and breathed her job."

"How did Tiffany find out Tyler had a wife?"

"In the worst of ways. Tyler's wife figured it out, and she

went to Tiffany's workplace and confronted her while she was in a work meeting with one of her colleagues, Everett."

"Do you know anything about their conversation?"

Ron pressed a hand to his throat, clearing it once, then a second time. "Hey … ahh, Foley. You mind getting me a soda? Should be some cans of lemon lime in the fridge."

He nodded, saying nothing as he walked toward the kitchen.

"The wife's name is Jana," Ron said. "At first, Tiffany worried the woman came to her office to create a scene, but she didn't. She just wanted to talk, woman to woman. After Tiffany learned Tyler had been unfaithful, she explained she had no idea Tyler had a wife."

"Did Jana believe her?"

"Tiffany thought she did. They talked for a while longer, and when Jana left, they'd even hugged each other."

"Did Tiffany ever see or speak to Jana again?"

"To my knowledge, no."

"How did Jana find out about the affair?" I asked.

"I don't know. She didn't say, as far as I know."

"Is Tyler aware this happened?"

"Jana confronted him right after she saw Tiffany."

"How did he react?"

"He admitted to it, and then he asked for a divorce."

Foley returned with a can of soda, which he handed to Ron.

"This Tyler fellow sounds like a stand-up guy," Foley muttered with a smirk.

"Strange thing is, I thought he was," Ron said.

"You've met Tyler?" I asked.

"Yeah, Tiffany invited me over for dinner one night, and he was here."

"What was your first impression of him?"

"I thought he was great. He was polite, and he asked me a

lot of questions about myself and my life. When he learned I like to play pool, he suggested we get together for a few games sometime. I have to say, in the short time we chatted with each other, he won me over … well, until I learned he's a dishonest bastard. Makes me wonder what other secrets the man's been keeping."

I wondered the same thing.

"Do you know what happened after Tyler asked Jana for a divorce?" I asked.

"He went straight to Tiffany's house and apologized for not telling her sooner. He begged her not to end their relationship. He said he'd asked Jana for a divorce so they could be together."

"How did Tiffany respond?"

"She had such strong feelings for him, his pleading almost worked, but I talked to her, helped her come to her senses. Once a liar, always a liar, in my opinion. Can't trust a guy who lies right out of the gate—no siree."

I now had two possible suspects, a great way to start my investigation.

I wondered, though … had Jana's understanding attitude the day she confronted Tiffany been genuine, or had it all been for show?

And Tyler, when the begging and pleading failed to win Tiffany back, had something darker taken hold, a different man rising up inside him, a man driven by rage?

Perhaps he loved Tiffany in a deceitful, unhealthy way.

Or …

I envisioned a scenario where Tyler was a faithful husband, a man who never planned to step out on his wife. Then he met Tiffany. They hit it off, and in time, he succumbed to temptation, taking a bite from the forbidden apple.

It made me question what his marriage had been like prior

to the affair and if he was planning on getting a divorce before he met Tiffany.

As the various scenarios ran through my mind, Ron wagged a finger at me. "Care to share what's on your mind?"

"Tyler and Jana make great suspects."

"Given I've never met the woman, I wouldn't know about Jana. It's true, Tyler makes a good suspect, though he's a half-pint, no taller than five-eight, weighs a buck fifty, if that. I'm not trying to say he didn't do it. I'm just giving you the facts."

Even half-pints could wield a knife.

And right now, Tyler was at the top of my suspect list.

11

It took some time to talk Ron into going home and getting some rest, but after I promised to keep him updated, he made his exit, giving me the chance to look over the rest of the house. My last stop was the one place I didn't want to go, even though I had to—the room where Tiffany had taken her last breath.

I reached for the doorknob, pausing before I turned it.

"I'm still not so sure about you going in there," Whitlock said from behind me. "I'm not trying to stand in your way, just want you to take a second. I'm just looking out for ya, is all."

"You know this is something I have to do, right? I'm sure I've seen other crime scenes that were a lot worse. And besides, she's not in there anymore."

He mumbled something under his breath, then said, "I suppose you're right."

As determined as I was to go inside, my stomach had other plans—churning sour, like I'd swallowed something that didn't sit right.

I took a moment to gather myself and then opened the door.

What hit me next was the blood—everywhere—and a scattering of numbered evidence markers.

"You okay, kiddo?" Whitlock asked.

He was standing beside me now, eyeing me with concern.

"For a moment, I thought I might lose my lunch, but I'm hoping it will pass," I said.

"Can I answer any questions for you?"

I glanced around the room, taking it all in.

"Tell me about these markers," I said. "What did you find?"

He pointed to the one closest to where we were standing. "Number one is where we found the knife. Two was a glass. Three her hairbrush. Four, a sock."

"A single sock?"

He nodded. "Yes, ma'am. We looked around for a mate and didn't find it. We're assuming it's hers, though. We found an identical pair in her dresser drawer. On her bed, she'd laid out a sundress, and there was a bra on top of it."

I pointed at marker number five, which was beside the toilet. "What was there?"

"Liquid of some kind. We'll have to wait for Silas to test it before we know more."

"Tell me about the consistency."

"My best guess? It's lotion. The bottom drawer was open when we arrived, and a bottle of lotion was sticking out with the lid flipped up. A bit of lotion had spilled onto the container, which could have then dripped onto the floor."

It made sense.

"Are there any stab marks on the back of her body?" I asked.

He shook his head. "Her wounds were on her front and sides."

Another wave of nausea hit me, harder than before, and this time, I wasn't sure I could keep everything down. Not wanting to sully the crime scene, I jerked back, sprinting out of the room and running smack-dab into Giovanni in the hallway.

He took hold of my arms and said, "Are you all right?"

"I need to … I need a bathroom."

I jerked free of his grip and ran down the hallway to the guest bathroom, throwing up not once, not twice, but three times. A few minutes later, the bathroom door opened a crack, and Giovanni slid a mug of peppermint tea inside.

"When you're ready, sip on this," he said. "I'm right here, right outside the door if you need me."

A half hour went by, then an hour, and I remained there, huddled in a corner on the floor, my face pressed into my knees as I sobbed, the reality of Tiffany's death settling in.

I would never see her shining face again.

Not today.

Not tomorrow.

Not ever.

As I sat there, gutted and broken, I heard muffled voices in the hallway. Men, whispering like they thought their lowered voices would keep me from overhearing what they were saying. It didn't work, and I clung on to their every word.

"She's been in there for over an hour?" Foley asked. "I've never seen her react this way to a murder before. Then again, this one lands hard. Not easy, losing a friend."

"I was with her in Tiffany's bathroom," Whitlock said. "She seemed fine, at first. I don't think she's allowed herself to slow down enough to take it all in before now."

"Might be good for her, to get it all out," Foley said. "Is there anything we can do to help, Giovanni?"

It went quiet, and then Giovanni said, "We're here, showing our support, which is what she needs right now. When she's ready, she'll work through it in her own way."

It was the perfect response, and given he wasn't whispering, I was sure he knew I was listening.

"You think maybe I should try talking to her about not pushing herself to work the case with us?" Foley asked. "Might be best if she sits this one out."

Might be best for me to sit it out?

I think not.

"I'm not sitting anything out," I shouted. "I'm fine. I just needed a minute."

Or sixty.

"All right, all right," Foley said through the closed door. "Didn't mean to offend you. We'll ... ahh, I'll leave you to do, well, whatever it is you're doing."

It went quiet again, and then I heard a woman's voice, and I knew things were about to change.

There was more whispering, only this time I couldn't make out what was being said. The bathroom door opened. Hands on hips, my mother looked down at me, her expression telling me she was in full problem-solving mode.

"Well, aren't you a sight," she said.

I thought about making a witty comeback, but for once, I didn't have one.

Maybe everyone was right in saying I wasn't in the frame of mind I needed to be in to work this case.

I didn't feel like myself.

I felt like the farthest thing from it.

Was everyone else right, and I was wrong?

What if me being involved made things worse, not better?

What if ...

My mother cocked her head to the side and reached out a hand. "It's time to get up off the floor, dear. *You're* coming with me."

12

Five minutes later, I was sitting in the passenger seat of my mother's car, listening to her hum along to Post Malone's song "Sunflower," which was playing on the radio.

"He always makes you feel a little bit better, no matter what kind of day you're having, doesn't he?"

"Who?"

"Post Malone."

"I had no idea you were a fan of his music."

"I'm a big fan. Harvey put all his songs on a playlist for me. I listen to it a few times a week, or more. His words, they're good for the soul, kinda like that young lady …" She snapped her fingers. "Shoot, I can't think of her name just now … Bettie or Billie something."

"Billie Eilish."

"Yes, that's the one."

"Where are we going?" I asked.

"You'll see."

"Can't you just tell me?"

"Now listen, I know you're not one for surprises, but every

once in a while, don't you think it would be nice to relax and allow someone else to plan something for you?"

The mere thought ticked my anxiety up a notch.

"It's been a rough day," I said. "I just want to go home, open a bottle of wine, and quiet my mind."

"And you will ... *after* we stop at a fun little place first."

Looking out the window, we were getting farther away from Cambria, which meant I wasn't going home any time soon.

Another fifteen minutes, and my mother pulled to a stop, parking in front of a business called Shatterdays.

"Where are we?" I asked.

"We're in Morro Bay, of course."

"Yes, I know what city we're in. What is Shatterdays?"

My mother grinned, eyes glistening as she said, "It's a rage room, a place people go to smash the living hell out of things. You ready?"

I'd heard of places like this, where people went to vent their frustration, work through their anger, or just indulge in a bit of fun. I wasn't sure I was up to it. Whether I was or not, there was no way she was letting me sit this one out.

We exited the car and entered the building, choosing the "Break for Two" package amongst the list of choices. It was a ten-minute experience that would allow us to smash and shatter plates, cups, wine bottles, and even picture frames. We were handed a couple of baseball bats and bags containing face shields, hard hats, jumpsuits, gloves, and boots. Then we were escorted to our own private room.

When the door closed behind us, my mother said, "Time starts now, better get smashing!"

I stood a moment, taking it all in, still feeling unsure.

"All right, then," my mom prompted. "How about I start us out?"

Wielding the bat over her head, she walked to the other side of the room and unleashed on a series of wine bottles, sending shards and fragments everywhere. Witnessing the pure bliss she was in, I burst out laughing.

"That's the spirit!" my mother said. "Now put some of that inner rage to the test and show me what you got."

What started out as an activity I felt forced to participate in soon become an exercise I couldn't wait to get in on. I took aim at a set of plates, smashing them to pieces, thinking about Tiffany and the killer, the plates representing his face.

It was like an addictive drug.

The more I smashed, the better I felt.

"Whoo-eee!" my mother shouted. "That's my girl. Let it out. Let it *all* out."

And I did.

"I'm angry," I said.

"*Why* are you angry? Talk to me. Tell me how you're feeling."

I moved to a pile of teacups, annihilating the entire row. "I want the killer to suffer, to die the same way she did—hurting and in pain."

"Good, what else?"

"I want her back, even though I know I can't get her back. And I want to rewind time, find a way to prevent the murder from happening."

"You may not get to see her again, not in this lifetime, but you *will* catch the person responsible. When you do, you'll make sure they never hurt anyone ever again. Tiffany will have the justice she deserves, and you're going to get it for her."

"Justice won't bring her back."

"Maybe not, but it will give you closure, her father too, I expect."

"I don't want closure." I swiped at a wall of plates, sending every piece flying, then let my bat fall to my side. "I want her to be alive."

I leaned against the wall, allowing my emotions to rise within me, as I faced them head-on. "I just ... I don't know if I'm equipped to deal with it all right now."

My mother narrowed her eyes, then walked over to me. "What are you saying?"

"As determined as I am to investigate Tiffany's murder, Foley and Whitlock may be right about me letting them take the reins on this one."

"Since when have you ever let someone else's opinion stop you from doing what needs to be done?"

"I'm not in the best headspace right now."

"My goodness. I can't believe what I'm hearing. You're tough, Georgiana, and you're strong, even when you're facing a mountain of obstacles. You always find your way around, over, or through it. Now isn't the time to stop believing in yourself. You may be married to Giovanni, but you're still a Germaine, and we don't back down from anything."

All day I'd felt a strange sense of disconnection from myself, almost like I was going against my nature, against the grain of who I was as a person. It almost felt like I was outside of my own body, looking at a girl who in this moment had lost her way, her strength, her mojo. It was a wretched, horrible feeling, and I wanted nothing more than to rid myself of it.

My mother placed a reassuring hand on my shoulder. "Remember when Lark was kidnapped? You didn't hesitate to return home and hunt down the man who'd taken her. You lit a fire in yourself. You did it then, and you'll do it now."

In the past, my mother had always worried about me investigating murders, to the point where she often tried to talk me into choosing a different career, one that wasn't so dangerous.

Today, she was the opposite—encouraging me in a way she never had before.

"I always thought you'd jump at the chance for me to be anything other than a private detective," I said.

"I'm your mother, and I'll always worry, but I've also always known you're where you need to be, doing the exact thing you're meant to do. It wouldn't be right for me to hold you back. So, how do you feel now?"

"Different. Better."

It was true.

I did feel better, and I felt something else ... something even more rewarding.

My fire was lit, and I was ready to catch a killer.

13

The next morning, I met Simone and Hunter at the office to talk about our new investigation. Both ladies were former detectives I'd brought on when I formed the Case Closed Detective Agency a few years earlier. Since then, we'd solved a handful of homicide cases, Simone often speaking to the suspects I couldn't always get to, and Hunter researching behind the scenes. We made a good team, and no matter how much of a knack I had for catching criminals, the business wouldn't be where it was today without them.

When they joined me on the sofa, lattes in hand, I noticed they were a bit quieter than usual. When the silence became too stifling, I piped up with, "All right, look, I already have everyone else tiptoeing around me like they think I might break. I can't have you two doing it too. If we need to talk about what happened to Tiffany first and how I'm feeling about it so we can move on, then let's do it."

"I'm sorry," Hunter said.

"You don't need to be sorry," I replied. "I know you're concerned about me. Everyone is, and I appreciate it. No matter how personal this is to me, we have a job to do."

"We're just worried," Simone said. "That's all."

"About what?"

She leaned back, taking a sip of her latte as she crossed one leg over the other. "Maybe *worried* isn't the right word. We feel bad that you lost such a good friend. You two have known each other forever, and I'm sure her death is weighing on you."

"You're right," I said. "There is a heaviness that's been hard to shake."

"And hey, we don't have to talk about it if you don't want to, okay? We can get straight to the case. I know talking about your feelings isn't always the easiest thing for you."

Discussing my feelings with others had always felt like performing on stage without a script. It was weird and awkward, and I never felt like I said the right thing in the right way—if, in fact, there was a right way.

Hunter lifted a finger.

"What is it?" I asked.

"I feel like we need to admit that we know about what happened yesterday at Tiffany's house—you know, when you threw up and stuff."

Simone shot Hunter an irritated look like she'd just sold them out.

"What?" Hunter asked. "If we're sitting here telling her we're worried, she deserves to know why."

"It's fine," I said. "Continue."

"Okay, so Foley stopped by this morning before you got here. He was looking for you, and he ... well, he told us about you being in the bathroom. I should add that right after it came out of his mouth, he felt bad for saying it."

"How do you know he felt bad? Did he say as much?"

"Not with words, no. I could just tell."

And I could tell a lot of assumptions were flying around.

If I wanted to shift the conversation to investigating

Tiffany's murder, it seemed I was first going to have to share where my head was at.

I set my notebook and pen on my lap, my latte on the coffee table, and crossed my arms. "I'm going to explain what happened at Tiffany's house and why it did. Once I do, I'd like us to all move on, focus on what matters right now. And it isn't me."

They leaned a bit closer, eager to hear what I had to say.

"I was in a state of shock yesterday, right from the start. After we flew back, Whitlock was waiting for me at the airport. He gave me a ride to Tiffany's house, and before I went in, we talked for a while."

"About what?" Simone asked.

"Information they knew up to that point. I felt I'd handled the conversation well, and I convinced myself I was in the right headspace. Maybe I was at first. I then spoke with Tiffany's father at the house, and that conversation also went as well as it could have gone."

"When did things change?"

"I was in Tiffany's bathroom, taking in the murder scene, and I don't know ... I just felt like I was losing it. I ran from there to the guest bathroom, and I threw up a few times. Then I sat there on the floor, questioning whether to take the case or not. Foley and Whitlock suggested I let them be in the driver's seat, and you know me well enough to know when that happens, I always push back. This time it was different, though."

"We'd feel the same way if we were in your position," Hunter said. "And we want you to know we're here for you, for whatever you need."

What I needed was to wrap up the conversation about me and get to talking about how we were going to solve Tiffany's murder.

"I was … I mean I *am* grieving," I said. "And it's fine. If I have to grieve myself through this case, so be it. If I want to work it, there isn't another option."

"We … ahh, we also heard you left with your mother," Simone said. "I know how your mother can be sometimes, which worried me even more."

"You know something? There are these rare moments when she shines in times of turmoil, and she becomes a radiant beacon, instead of a stubborn, obstinate worrywart. Yesterday, she was the beacon. She gave me a pep talk, reminded me of who I am, who we are, and why we do what we do."

"Wow," Simone said. "Go, Darlene. I'm impressed."

"I was too. She may not always like the investigations we take, but she showed me a level of support yesterday I never expected. I slept on it, woke up this morning as determined as ever, and now we're all here."

"I'm glad you decided we should be involved."

"Me too," Hunter said. "Where do we start?"

Reaching for my notebook and pen, I grinned, pleased to be getting the ball rolling.

"Let's start with a few notes I've taken," I said. "In the months before Tiffany died, she was dating someone new, a man named Tyler Seymour. When she talked to me about him, she gave me the impression he was different than the other guys she'd dated, a man she could see a future with one day."

"How long did they date?" Hunter asked.

"Several months, but right before our wedding, they broke up."

"Why?"

"Turns out, Tyler's married."

"Holy crap," Hunter said. "Didn't see that one coming."

"Me neither," I said. "The wife, Jana, found out her husband was having an affair, and she confronted Tiffany at her law office."

"The woman's got balls," Simone said. "Sounds like we have ourselves a great suspect."

"More like *two* suspects," Hunter added. "What's the husband's story? Why did he decide to have an affair? Not to mention the risks involved in lying to both his wife and Tiffany. That never ends well. What was he thinking?"

"All good questions I don't have answers for yet. I plan to speak to them both today. I'll tell you what I know so far, but until I hear their stories, let's not assume anything."

"Even when you talk to them, you might not know if they're lying to you," Hunter said.

"Oh, there are ways, little tells sometimes."

"I've never been any good at knowing when a person is lying."

Hunter could be a bit too trusting, but when it came to looking into a person's background, she was a tech ninja.

"Let's go over what I know about Tyler so far," I said. "He is a real estate agent, and he was helping Tiffany find an investment rental. At some point during that process, they hit it off and started dating."

"Until the wife found out, I bet," Simone said.

"Here's something interesting. When Jana confronted Tiffany at work, I expected to hear that she was erratic, which is common in these situations. I was told she was calm and collected, talking to Tiffany like she didn't place any of the blame on her. She put it all on Tyler. She and Tiffany even hugged at the end."

Shocked, Simone shook her head. "What happened after their lovey powwow?"

"The wife told Tyler she knew about the affair, and

according to Tiffany's father, Tyler told Jana he wanted a divorce."

"I don't get it. If he wanted a divorce, why make it so messy? He could have done the right thing and asked for the divorce *before* he started dating Tiffany. Maybe if he had, it all would have gone down a different way."

"Who knows? People cheat for a lot of reasons."

Hunter scrunched up her face, nodding. "Yeah, like the thrill of the chase and the fact it feels so naughty. Brings in an extra level of excitement for some people."

Simone tipped her head back, laughing. "Umm, Hunter, is there anything you'd like to tell us?"

"Oh, no. Come on. I wouldn't ever … I just, I watch a lot of murder mysteries on television. Half the time, an affair has something to do with it."

Simone eyed Hunter like she questioned her answer.

"Ladies, let's get back on track," I said. "Tyler and Jana are the first people on my list to question, though to accuse them now seems too easy. If either one of them murdered Tiffany, they would have known they'd be a prime suspect. I'll see what they have to say, and then we'll discuss their statements. In the meantime, Hunter, I'd like you to look into Tiffany's recent clients. Her last legal case was a bit rough on her. I'd like to know more about it."

"You bet. What type of case was it?"

"Divorce. She handled a lot of them. Given she won almost every case she took on, I'm wondering if there's something there."

"Are you thinking there might be a disgruntled husband?"

"I am."

I turned toward Simone. "I'd like you to talk to Tiffany's neighbors. See if they saw or heard anything on the day of the murder. I'm sure Foley and Whitlock have already spoken to them, but it wouldn't hurt to circle back and speak to them ourselves."

"I'm on it," she said.

And with that, it was go time.

14

I stepped into the real estate office where Tyler worked and made my way to the front desk, where a young woman with curly red hair and a sprinkle of freckles looked up at me. Her nametag read *Lila*.

"Hello, Lila," I said. "I would like to speak with Tyler Seymour. Is he here?"

She shook her head. "He hasn't been in yet today."

I glanced at a mid-century metal sunburst clock on the wall, noting the time. It was eleven o'clock on a Monday, and given realtors often had flexible schedules, the fact he wasn't there didn't concern me—at first.

"Do you know when Tyler will be in today?" I asked.

"I don't."

She looked past me, eyeing the cars in the parking lot, and frowned.

"Is everything all right?" I asked.

"Yeah ... it's just, Tyler often gets to work before me most days. He missed a meeting with one of his clients this morning."

"Was the meeting important?"

"I'd say so. His client was supposed to be signing the real estate paperwork for a new house."

"Does Tyler miss meetings like this often?"

"No, never."

I wondered where he was and why he was a no-show.

"Did you try calling him?" I asked.

"Of course, I did."

"And?"

"It rang a few times and then went to voicemail, so I sent him a text message. He responded, saying he was running late, and had asked Jordan to step in." She reached out, straightening a few papers on her desk. "I'm sorry."

"For what?"

"I shouldn't have told you what I just did. Bad habit, I guess. I get too chatty sometimes, and it gets me in trouble. Do you want me to leave Tyler a message?"

"Will you tell him Georgiana Germaine stopped by?"

She scribbled my name down on a notepad. "Does he have your number?"

"Not yet. I'm here to talk to him about one of his clients, Tiffany Wheeler."

"Why?"

"I'm a private investigator."

Lila's eyes widened. "Oh. Shoot."

She clammed up, her focus shifting from me to the computer in front of her.

But I wasn't finished with her yet.

"Who's Jordan?" I asked.

"I am."

I turned and saw a bald, middle-aged man leaning against an office doorway, his arms crossed in front of him. He was dressed in a white polo shirt, gray slacks, and shiny, copper-colored loafers. "Is there something I can do for you, Miss ...?"

"It's Mrs., and yes, you can start by telling me why Tyler asked you to do his job this morning."

He glanced around, looking uncomfortable. "We should talk in my office."

I followed him down the hall and into his office. He shut the door behind us, then pointed at a set of chairs, saying, "Please, take a seat."

I sat and looked around.

On his desk, a few file folders were stacked in a neat pile. Beside them were a couple of framed photos—one of a labrador retriever and another of Audrey Hepburn arm in arm with Fred Astaire. There was also a mug with the name of the real estate office on the front. Inside it were several pens, pencils, and a travel-sized bottle of hand sanitizer.

Shifting my attention from the desk to a box sitting on the floor behind it, I said, "That's a big box of candles."

He sat across from me, tapping his foot against the floor. "I use them in my open houses. The scent creates an inviting atmosphere, makes it smell homey and lived in. Tyler is a good friend, a *close* friend. Why are you here asking questions?"

"Tiffany Wheeler was *my* close friend."

"What does that have to do with Tyler?"

"Tiffany was murdered, or haven't you heard?"

His smug grin faded, replaced by a look of sadness. "Yeah, I heard. I expect the entire town's buzzing about it by now."

I hesitated a moment, trying to decide which direction to take the conversation in next. As much as I wanted to push, I realized a slow start might be better.

"Tyler was Tiffany's real estate agent," I said. "I understand he was helping her find a house to buy. Were you aware he was working with her?"

"I was, yes, though there's not much I can tell you. I met her once when she dropped by the office to meet Tyler. We spoke for a few minutes, just light chitchat. I thought she was a nice woman, an attractive one too. I was shocked when I heard about what happened to her."

"I understand the meeting Tyler missed this morning was an important one."

He shrugged. "Whatever Lila told you ... well, she tends to exaggerate. It's not a big deal. I handled it. We stand in for each other from time to time."

"Did Tyler say why he missed the meeting?"

"In his text message he said something came up, and he couldn't make it to work on time."

"Did he give you any other information?"

"He didn't, and I didn't ask. Like I said before, it's no big deal. I'm here, and I was happy to help."

"Did his clients seem bothered that he wasn't available?"

"I explained he had a personal emergency, and they were fine."

"But you don't *know* if he had a personal emergency, do you?"

Jordan leaned back. "I mean, no ... but he could have had one."

"So, you lied to his clients."

"I did what I thought was best. I covered for him the best I could, and it all worked out."

"Since you're here and Tyler's not, I have a few questions," I said. "Tyler and Tiffany were—"

"I think it would be best if you waited and talked to Tyler."

He'd interrupted me, a fact I decided to overlook, for now.

"When I was speaking to Lila a few minutes ago, did you hear our conversation?" I asked.

"Most of it. I heard you say you're a private investigator."

"I am. I'm also assisting the police with their investigation."

"Again, I'm not sure how I can help."

"You said Tyler's a close friend. I assume you know a fair bit about his private life. Don't you?"

"I mean, we're men. We don't go into all the details about our lives outside the workplace. We hang out sometimes, grab a few beers, that kind of thing."

He'd shifted from portraying Tyler as a close friend to downplaying their connection, now referring to him like he was an acquaintance.

"Has Tyler ever talked to you about Tiffany?" I asked.

"Why would he?"

Jordan was playing coy, and I couldn't decide if he knew about the affair or not. I was about to mention it when he sighed, looking me in the eye as he said, "Aside from working with Tiffany to find a house, she was a client, just like any other client."

Unless Tyler made a habit of sleeping with many of his female clients, she was a lot more than that, and I'd grown tired of Jordan's deflections.

"Did you know Tiffany and Tyler were having an affair?" I asked.

"I ... to be honest, no," he stuttered. "Where are you getting your information from?"

"I had lunch with Tiffany before she died, and she told me she was in a relationship with Tyler. At the time, she didn't know he was married. Do you think I'm misinformed?"

"I've known Tyler and Jana for years. I'm not sure why your friend told you what she did, but I don't believe it."

It was obvious I was pushing buttons he didn't want pushed, and based on the look on his face, he was just about at his breaking point.

"I get why you believe she was telling you the truth, given she was your friend and all," he said. "To me, it makes no sense."

It was about to ...

I leaned forward, looking him in the eye. "Given Tyler is your *close* friend, I understand why you're being protective and covering for him."

"I'm not."

"You know what's interesting about my job? I'm good at reading people. It helps me know when to turn up the heat with someone I'm questioning, or when to tone it down. I often know when a person is lying to me."

Up to now, he'd kept his cool, but after my last comment, his expression soured. "I don't like what you're insinuating."

"And I don't like that you're lying to me."

Shaking his head, he said, "This conversation is over."

Over for him, perhaps.

Not for me.

"Let's go over the facts," I said. "You've been tapping your foot on the floor nonstop for the last ten minutes. And then there are the words you've chosen to use, words like 'to be honest.' These are just a couple of indicators that a person is lying."

He tipped his head toward his office door. "I'd like you to leave now, unless you'd rather I call the police and tell them I'm being harassed."

Crossing one leg over the other, I said, "What a marvelous idea. Go right ahead."

"What?"

"I said—Go. Right. Ahead."

"Fine ... I—"

"Maybe between all of us we can get to the truth. There's something I haven't told you. Tiffany's father had dinner with her before she died, and he met Tyler. I didn't mention it before because I wanted to give you a chance to be honest with me."

"I ... well, I ..."

"I'm not finished yet. You can lie to me and get away with it, but if you lie to the police, you're breaking the law. Here's another fact. Tyler's wife knows about the affair. She confronted Tiffany at work, and they discussed it. So, what do you say, Jordan? Shall we try again?"

15

Jordan excused himself for a moment, leaving the office and returning with a variety of soda options. Setting them on the desk, he looked at me, gesturing to the drink offerings as he asked if I wanted anything. I didn't have soda often, but today my throat was dry. Thinking something fizzy might help, I reached for the orange flavor and cracked it open, thanking him.

He grabbed one for himself and sat back down.

"I owe you an apology," he said. "I've been friends with Tyler for many years, and I'm sorry if I wasn't honest with you. It's not who I am, but this situation has left me in a bit of a predicament. I could have handled it better, and I didn't."

"You were trying to protect him. I get it."

"I also wasn't aware the news about Tyler and Tiffany's relationship had gotten out."

"What do you know about the affair?"

He set the can of soda on the desk, tapping a finger against the can, thinking. "I realize my dishonesty has left you with no reason to trust me, but believe me when I say, if you're thinking

Tyler had anything to do with the death of your friend, he did not."

It was just what a person protecting their friend would say, preferring to see them in the best possible light instead of entertaining the notion everyone had a breaking point—even Tyler.

"How long have you known about the affair between Tyler and Tiffany?" I asked.

"Not long. Tyler came into work one morning, and right away, I could tell something was off. Most days, the first thing he does when he gets here is to come to my office and greet me. That day, he went to his office and shut the door, even though he knew I was here."

"Did you speak to him?"

"Yeah, I went to his office and tried to make small talk. He told me he hadn't been sleeping well, but he didn't say why."

"You didn't ask?"

"Maybe I should have, but no, I didn't. A few days later, when I got to work, he was sitting in my office, waiting for me to get here. That's when he told me about Tiffany."

At long last, we were getting somewhere.

Now I just needed to keep him talking.

"What did Tyler say about their relationship?"

"I don't think I should keep talking about it. I feel uncomfortable, like I'd be betraying his trust any more than I already have."

"If the police haven't already spoken to Tyler, they will, and they'll ask the same questions I'm asking you now. Whether the truth comes out today or tomorrow, it doesn't matter. It *will* come out."

"Even if it does, I'd feel a whole lot better if it came from him, not me."

I may not have liked his answer, but I respected it.

I decided to take a different approach, changing the subject in hopes of finding a way to circle back, asking the same question but in a different way, a tactic I called the Dodge and Confuse.

"Do you know why Tyler hasn't turned up for work yet today and why he wasn't here to meet his client?" I asked. "Not being here for a client isn't a good look."

"All I know is what I've already told you."

"Still, you must have thought it was odd, given Lila told me Tyler often gets to work before she does in the morning."

"I didn't question why he couldn't be here, but I did ask if everything was all right. He said we'd talk later. Beyond that, I didn't press him for details." He paused, then added, "I suppose it's my turn to ask you a question. What can you tell me about Jana's meeting with Tiffany?"

"They had an open, honest conversation, from what I've been told. Afterward, Jana confronted Tyler. She confessed she knew about the affair and told him she'd been to see Tiffany. He asked Jana for a divorce. Then he went to see Tiffany. He told her he'd asked for a divorce, and he tried to keep her from ending their relationship, but she did anyway. Speaking of their relationship, I don't know much about it. Anything you could tell me would help."

Jordan raised a brow. "Before I knew about Tiffany, I thought Tyler's relationship with Jana was solid. Then he admitted to falling in love with Tiffany, said he was struggling with what to do about it."

For all we knew, he could have been having an affair with multiple women.

"I didn't know he'd fallen in love with her," I said. "She felt he was someone she could have a future with, until she learned about Jana."

"I was shocked when he told me. It didn't seem like the Tyler I know."

"What doesn't sound like the Tyler you know?"

I'd been so involved in our conversation, I hadn't realized the office door had just opened, and Jordan and I were no longer alone. I turned, recognizing Tyler from photos Tiffany had shown me.

He looked disheveled, like he'd been running his fingers through his hair all day. His collared shirt wasn't buttoned right, with one side hanging lower than the other. And his eyes were red and bloodshot, full of emotion.

Upon seeing Tyler, Jordan rose from his chair, his voice low and sheepish as he walked toward him.

"Hey, bud, how's it going?" Jordan asked.

Tyler shrugged him off, glaring at him.

Then he turned his attention on me.

"Who are you?" Tyler asked. "And why are the two of you sitting here talking about me?"

"It's not what you think," Jordan said. "We weren't talking about you. Well ... that is to say, we were, but it was just a casual conversation. I can explain."

"Sounds to me like this woman just said something about me, and you didn't disagree."

Jordan shot me a nervous look, like he wasn't sure how to get himself out of his current predicament.

"Maybe I should start by telling you my name," I said. "I'm Georgiana Germaine."

Tyler blinked at me. "I've heard of you before ... I just don't know from where."

"If I had to guess, Tiffany told you about me," I said.

"*Tiffany?*"

"Tiffany Wheeler, your former client."

"Ah, yes, *that* Tiffany."

It was a laidback remark, like she was someone he didn't know well.

"I'm a private investigator," I said. "And given Tiffany was one of my close friends, I'm involved in the investigation of her murder. I came here this morning hoping to talk to you, but you weren't here, so I chatted with Jordan in the meantime."

"A chat about me, by the sounds of it. As far as Tiffany's murder, I don't have any information that will help you or the police."

It had taken me so long to get anywhere with Jordan, I didn't have the mental capacity to go another round—this time with Tyler.

"Can we skip the part where you tell me you didn't know her well or not on a personal level, and just get to the point?" I asked. "You were having an affair with her. She told me, her father told me. Her father also said the two of you have met, when you all had dinner together."

Tyler leaned against the wall, crossing his arms in front of him. "You're right, but I wouldn't call it an affair."

"What would you call it, then?"

"I'm not sure I can think of the right words to explain what we were doing, but it was real. To me, anyway. What else do you know?"

"Your wife went to see Tiffany to tell her she knew about the affair. Then she talked to you, and according to her, you asked for a divorce. You then tried to salvage what you had with Tiffany, but you failed, and she ended the relationship."

He didn't respond, just stood there gnawing on his lower lip.

I waited.

Some time passed, then he said, "Everything you just said is correct, with the exception of one thing."

"And what's that?"

"She may have ended the relationship, but I thought I could win her back over time."

"How can you be so sure?"

"Because the last time we spoke, she told me she still loved me."

16

As more customers and real estate agents slipped in and out of the office, Tyler's discomfort level grew. To keep the conversation going, I suggested the two of us finish talking within the safe confines of my car. He hesitated at first, but he also seemed to understand I wasn't leaving until my questions were answered.

He slid into the seat beside me, downing a bottle of water he'd brought along, which he tossed on the floor like he hadn't been raised with a stitch of manners.

I wasted no time digging in.

"Where were you when Tiffany died?" I asked.

"Taking down a couple real estate signs and putting a new one up at one of my listings."

"Did anyone see you?"

"I'm sure they did. If I need an alibi to prove my innocence, I shouldn't have a problem getting one."

I switched subjects.

"I'm unclear about what your intentions were with Tiffany," I said.

"In what way?"

"In *all* ways."

"Can you be more specific?"

I could.

I just wasn't sure he was ready for it.

"Not disclosing the fact that you're married means you deceived her from the start," I said. "Tiffany was a charming, wonderful woman, but sometimes she could be a bit too trusting, a trait certain men picked up on when they dated her. She'd been taken advantage of more than once by the guys she dated —*including you.*"

"It was never my intention to deceive her. I felt awful about it from the start."

"I did an internet search of your name this morning. It took me all of three minutes to find something that confirmed you're married. It would have been easy for Tiffany to do the same. I'm guessing she didn't because she trusted you. She believed in you. Whether you're guilty or innocent of her murder, you let her down, and I can't forgive you for that."

He ran a hand through his hair. "I know I wasn't straight with her. I've agonized over it for months."

"If you've been in agony, you brought it on yourself. In the end, she would have figured it out, and if she didn't, I would have figured it out for her."

"It's not like I didn't want to tell her the truth. I *couldn't.*"

"I disagree."

"I thought if I told her, she wouldn't give me a chance, give *us* a chance. So, yeah, I withheld that information. Days turned to weeks and then months, and the weight of it kept getting bigger. I'd wake up each morning fearing it would be the day she'd discover my secret. I'd say to myself, 'Today is the day you're going to tell her.' The day would come and go, and at the end of it, I couldn't bring myself to do it."

It felt like we were running circles around the same topic—

a past that couldn't be changed—and there were far more pressing questions I still hadn't gotten to yet.

"How did the two of you meet?" I asked.

"In the grocery store of all places. I was walking by, and I noticed she'd grabbed an armful of oranges. When she went to put them in her basket, most of them slipped out of her hands and onto the floor. I bent down to offer my help. We both leaned over at the same time and butted heads. After we had a good laugh about it, she stuck a hand out and told me her name. I gave her mine, and we shook hands. Then we started talking about what I did for a living."

It would have made an adorable story.

Kismet.

If he wasn't married.

Tyler drummed his fingers along the dashboard, then looked at me. "If the two of you were such good friends, why didn't she tell you how we met?"

It was a fair question.

When we'd gotten together for lunch, I was in full wedding-planning mode, and most of our conversations revolved around my big day. Thinking back on it now, I was riddled with some of the decisions I made that day.

When she started a new relationship, I often vetted the guy—without her knowledge, of course. With Tyler, I'd been so preoccupied with wedding planning, I didn't look into him.

Why?

Maybe because it was the happiest I'd seen her in a long time.

I wanted Tyler to be different than the rest.

I wanted her to have what *I* had with Giovanni.

And I thought—*what's the harm in backing off, allowing her a moment to enjoy herself before I stuck my nose into her business.*

Turned out, backing off was a bad idea.

I'd dropped the ball, and the hollow ache in my core was a constant reminder. I was so caught up in my feelings of guilt it took me a moment to notice Tyler had been eyeing me, looking confused. I realized he was witnessing one of my strange habits —the way my eyes glazed over when I was deep in thought, mentally checked out of a conversation.

"You all right?" he asked.

"Yeah, fine. Getting back to the first time you met, I'm guessing she hired you to be her real estate agent. Then what?"

"Hold on a minute. I asked you why you thought Tiffany didn't tell you about the way we met. You expect me to answer your questions, but you won't answer mine. Is that it?"

"Depends on the question. I'll say this ... Tiffany talked a lot about you that day. We also talked about other things. I had a wedding coming up and ... You know what? None of that matters. What matters is I was aware of your relationship."

What I kept to myself was the fact I'd cut our lunch short that day because I had a dress fitting at the bridal shop. I could have rescheduled the fitting, and I didn't.

"When did you first realize you had feelings for Tiffany?" I asked.

"There was an immediate spark when we met at the grocery store. I didn't realize it at first, but when it hit me, there was no denying it."

"The spark couldn't have been strong, in my opinion, since you continued to juggle two relationships at the same time."

Tyler sighed and glanced out the window.

He looked disappointed, though not with me.

More with himself than anything.

"As hard as it is to believe, I've always had a tremendous amount of respect for my wife," he said.

"Have you ever cheated on her before?"

"No, never."

"How long have you been married?"

"Seven years."

The good ol' seven-year itch, a common lull in marriage where one often became restless, dissatisfied, and in need of something more—*someone* more. If given the opportunity to take hold, it had the ability to end marriages, as evidenced with this one.

"How long have you known your wife?" I asked.

"Fifteen years."

"Why did you wait so long to get married?"

"Our relationship was long distance for the first few years. Man ... you know something? You're good. I'm not the kind of person who talks about my private life often, let alone to someone I just met. I don't know what it is about you. I find myself wanting to tell you things. It's an odd feeling."

We cared about the same person. Maybe it created an instant bond for him, though I didn't share the sentiment.

"I've had a lot of practice interviewing people," I said. "Before I had my private detective agency, I was a police officer, then a detective."

"Why'd you leave to start something on your own?"

"Too much bureaucratic tape. I prefer working for myself, making my own rules."

"I get it. It's why I like real estate. Set my own hours, work at a pace of my choosing."

His career and why he'd chosen it was of no importance to me, so I steered things back in the right direction.

"I haven't had the chance to talk to your wife yet," I said. "What's she like?"

"I wouldn't say we've always had a great relationship, but we've always had a good one. Our marriage has had its share of ups and downs just like any other. No matter the issue, we always got through it. In the past, anyway."

"If your marriage was good, why risk it by starting something with someone else?"

"Have you ever met a person who swooped in when you least expected it and changed your entire world, your entire way of thinking?"

I thought back to the moment I'd first met Giovanni, then to the time we'd reconnected five years ago. And now married. After so many years apart, it didn't take long for me to realize I was meant to be with him all along. He'd "swooped" in on my heart from day one.

"I have someone like that in my life, but I didn't cheat on anyone to get him," I said.

It was harsh, and I knew it.

It was also true.

"I never planned to cheat on my wife," he said. "It just happened, and I ... I'm not sure how to even put it into words."

"Can you try?"

There was a long silence, then he said, "I have a feeling when our affair gets out, everyone is going to be looking at me, thinking I may have had something to do with Tiffany's murder. All I can tell you is, it wasn't me. And after meeting you today and seeing how tenacious you are, I'd rather have you in my corner than out of it."

A wise choice.

I didn't mind being in his corner for a time, *if* he was innocent.

If he was guilty, there would be a reckoning—swift and, perhaps, painful.

"You've told me more than I expected you would," I said. "The more I know, the more open I'll be to standing up for you, as long as you're honest with me, and you don't hold back."

"You'd asked me to put my feelings for Tiffany into words. All I can say is, the more I saw her, the more I was convinced she was the one for me. It felt like we were born to find each other, as if we'd lived multiple lives, and in each one, she was in it, and no matter what the odds, we'd always found each other somehow."

"When you realized how strong your feelings were, why didn't you do the right thing and come clean to Tiffany and to your wife?"

He shook his head. "You don't get it."

"What don't I get?"

"You don't know what it's like to be in this kind of predicament. You've never been through it."

"You have no idea what I've been through."

"I'm … you're right. Sorry. I just meant to say, when you care for two people at the same time, even if it's in different ways, the last thing you want to do is to hurt either of them."

"Your lies hurt them both."

"I was trying to find a way to be with Tiffany, to have a future together, while also considering Jana's happiness. It's all I thought about. All day. Every day."

The more he talked, the more it sounded like he was focusing on himself, his needs, and how *he'd* be affected.

"I'd like you to stop thinking about it from your perspective, what *you* wanted," I said. "Think about Tiffany and Jana, about how you would feel if they treated you the same way. Lied, cheated. If *you* had been the one on the receiving end, what then?"

He wiggled around in his seat like he was trying to get comfortable. "I'll admit, I didn't think of it that way, not until Tiffany expressed her feelings for me. I'll never forget it. We were walking through the park, and she told me she was falling in love with me. I'd felt the same way about her for weeks. But given my circumstances, I didn't know how to handle it, and I panicked."

"And you still didn't tell her the truth."

"I kept thinking I'd find a way past it, a way to smooth it over. As the days passed, I came up with ideas here and there, but none of them seemed right, so yeah, I kept stalling."

"How long were you planning on living a double life?"

"This is going to seem hard to believe, but the day my wife confronted me, I'd written her a letter, thinking it might be the best way to describe what had been going on."

It was hard to believe, the timing almost too perfect, and I questioned whether he was telling me the truth.

"Did you ever give her the letter?" I asked.

"I told her I'd written one. She didn't care to read it."

"How did your wife find out you were having an affair?"

"That is the million-dollar question." His cell phone rang inside his pocket. He pulled it out and looked at it, canceling the call and then setting the phone to the side. "I don't know how Jana found out. The only person I told was Jordan."

"Do you think he told her?"

"When she confronted me, I considered the possibility that he betrayed my confidence. But no, I don't think he did."

"Why not?"

"He's always been a good friend."

"Some friends have a way of turning on you in certain situations."

"Not Jordan. We go way back."

"You seemed upset with him earlier, when you thought we were talking about you."

"Yeah, that's because I didn't know who you were. Now that I do, it makes sense why the two of you were talking about me."

Maybe it made sense to him.

Not to me.

"If Jordan didn't speak to Jana, who did?" I asked.

"Beats me."

Although he'd been dishonest with both women, for the moment, I was willing to believe he didn't know how Jana learned about the affair. Thinking I had a better shot at getting it out of her, I didn't press the subject any further.

"Tell me about the day your wife confronted you," I said.

"She'd cooked me a pot roast for dinner, mashed potatoes and homemade biscuits—the works—which was unusual."

"How so?"

"It was my favorite comfort food, but Jana didn't like making it. We'd only have it on my birthday or on a special occasion. Most of the time, she preferred going to a restaurant instead of cooking dinner herself. As soon as we sat down to eat, she got straight to the point. She told me she knew Tiffany's name, where she worked, how we met, and all about my affair."

"What did you say in response?" I asked.

"All I wanted in that moment was to give a full confession, no matter how hard it might be for her to hear. I told her how sorry I was that everything happened the way it had, and I admitted I was in love with Tiffany. I even told her I thought Tiffany and I were meant to be together."

I couldn't decide if he was an idiot or thoughtless or a bit of both.

"What was your wife's reaction?" I asked.

"First, I want to say, I told Jana I still loved her, and I do. It's just ... the love I feel for her is different than my love for Tiffany."

"Please tell me you kept that part to yourself."

"I got the chance to tell the truth that night, and I went all in. I mean, why not? I was relieved to get it out. The relationship was over. I wanted us to appreciate the good times we had while accepting we were at our end. I thought if we could do that, we could heal, and we could both move on."

"How did Jana react?"

"Not in the way I expected. She threw a glass of red wine in my face, grabbed her keys, and she left."

In all my years as a detective, no one had ever been as candid with me as he just had. I was used to people evading me, telling me as little as possible, or nothing at all. When it came to the conversation with his wife, he seemed unemotional and disengaged, a different person than when we first started talking.

So different, in fact, I almost didn't know what to make of him.

17

I found Jana in a chair on the front porch, petting a dachshund draped across her lap with one hand, and holding a mug of coffee in the other. She was on the slender side and dressed in a long, flowy, multi-colored, tank top dress with sun symbols all over it. In terms of age, she was younger than I'd expected, several years younger than Tyler, I guessed. And with her long, dark hair, brooding eyes, and milky-white complexion, far more superior to him in looks.

I walked toward her, and she met my gaze, then set the mug she was holding down on a side table.

"Are you the private detective I've been hearing about?" she asked.

"I see word travels fast."

"Tyler texted me. He said you'd be coming."

"I was hoping to ask you a few questions."

She tipped her head to the side, gesturing at the chair next to her. "Take a seat."

I sat on a wicker chair with a red-and-orange striped cushion, surprised to find it was a lot more comfortable than I expected.

"What else did Tyler say when he messaged you?" I asked.

"He told me who you are, and he mentioned you and Tiffany were close friends. I'm guessing you spoke with him about his relationship with her."

"She is one of the reasons I went to see him, but he wasn't there when I first arrived, so I talked to Jordan. He lied to me about having any knowledge of the affair. Then I told him I knew about it, and when I gave him the facts, he changed his story."

She twisted the black bracelets she was wearing, nodding. "I'm sure he was just trying to protect his friend. We're all on edge. You can't tell me you wouldn't do the same thing if you were in our situation. Tyler and I both know we're suspects, though neither of us had anything to do with her murder."

"I'd refuse to answer a question I didn't want to answer. I wouldn't lie."

"Refusing to answer would seem suspicious."

She had a point.

And I was ready to move on.

"Who told you about Tyler and Tiffany?" I asked.

"*Tyler and Tiffany,*" she said, singing their names like they were lyrics in a song. "Rolls off the tongue like they go together, doesn't it? Not like Tyler and Jana, which has more of an oil and vinegar ring to it."

It was an odd comment, almost like she was paying them a compliment.

"To your question," she continued. "No one told me."

"If no one told you, how did you find out?"

She cracked a smile and reached for the mug. "I have my ways."

"Care to elaborate?"

"At the moment, no. I'd rather not."

Jana seemed open to me asking questions but closed to answering them.

She pointed at me. "See?"

"See what?"

"The way you just looked at me with a skeptical look on your face like you questioned my response. That's what I'm talking about. Refusing to answer your questions makes me look suspicious."

"I'll admit, it does."

As I contemplated what to say next, a scent, earthy and pine-like, filled the air. Incense, I guessed, wafting through an open window of her house.

"After I spoke to Jordan, I had a long conversation with Tyler," I said. "And based on the fact he told you I was coming over, it seems like the two of you are getting along all right."

"He's making more of an effort than I am."

"I heard when you confronted Tyler about the affair, he asked you for a divorce."

"Oh, I don't know about a divorce. We talked about a lot of things that night. We decided to separate, for now, to give him the chance to work through his feelings. I think he's confused and trying to figure out what he wants and doesn't want."

My head was spinning, questioning everything I'd been told so far—by everyone. What was true, what wasn't—gray areas I found frustrating.

Tyler was clear about his intention to get everything out in the open with Jana so he could move on with Tiffany. And yet, Jana was acting like there was a chance the relationship wasn't over.

Or maybe, she was telling herself what she wanted to believe.

"I'm confused," I said. "Tiffany's father told me Tyler tried to save his relationship with Tiffany after she found out he was married."

She ran a hand through her hair. "I don't know what to tell you."

"I feel like I'm getting two different stories."

She gave the dog another pat and said, "Maybe I'm worried you're going to try to pit us against each other, and I'm using caution with the words I choose to say."

The comment was laughable.

"I'm not," I said. "If you're both innocent, there's no reason for you not to be straight with me."

"You've just lost one of your closest friends. I'll bet you're desperate to solve her murder. You might not be thinking straight. If you're not, you could end up pinning her murder on the wrong person."

My frustration had gone from a simmer to a boil.

"Desperate is the last thing I am," I said. "Nor am I trying to pin Tiffany's murder on someone who's innocent. Why would I want to convict the wrong person? As for solving her murder—I *will* find out who killed her and why. So do yourself a favor and give me the facts."

"You want facts? Here's two. I didn't murder your friend. Tyler didn't either."

I leaned back, crossing my arms, trying to find a single iota of calm, which seemed out of reach.

"Here's what I've been told so far," I said. "Tyler made it clear to you on the night you made him the pot-roast dinner that he was meant to be with Tiffany, and his future was with her, not you."

"He said a lot of things that night. He was drunk."

An interesting side note he hadn't mentioned—*if* she was telling the truth.

"Drunk or not, he confessed his feelings for her," I said.

"He was just ... he wasn't himself. He's been a bit stressed over the past several months."

Juggling two women at the same time had a way of doing that to a person.

"If you ask me," Jana continued, "he would have never gone through with the divorce. She was just ... and hey, I'm sorry to say this given she was your friend and all, but she was just a bit of fun, a temporary placeholder while we went through a rough patch."

I was starting to think Jana was leaning toward the delusional side, creating her own truths so she didn't have to face the fact her marriage was over.

"If Tyler wasn't planning to leave you for Tiffany, he had no reason to admit his feelings for her to me," I said. "He could have said it was an affair, nothing more. I believe him, Jana."

"Believe what you want. I'll do the same."

"Where were you around the time Tiffany was murdered?"

"Having lunch with my mother."

"Where?"

She rolled her eyes. "Wherever the woman wants to go."

"And where did she want to go this last time?"

"Harvest Hollow. She's addicted to their chicken pecan sandwiches."

I didn't blame her.

They were the best sandwiches in town.

"When you mentioned your mother just now, you wrinkled your nose," I said.

"You don't miss a thing, do ya?"

"I wouldn't be great at my job if I did."

"We've never been close, but she keeps trying to force a relationship, like I can just forget about all the crap she put me through in the past, the constant revolving door of my childhood, men coming in and out. My needs were always pushed to the side. Now that she's older, her looks have faded, and she has few friends and even fewer lovers, she's decided I have meaning in her life."

"If you don't want a relationship, why meet with her?"

"Tyler thought if we fixed our relationship, I could let go of some of the things from the past."

"How's that working out?"

"It isn't."

"You don't strike me as the type of person to do something just because Tyler suggests it."

She set the mug back down and clapped her hands together. "Right again. My mother's unwell. Cancer. Figure I can manage a few visits here and there. She'll be gone soon enough."

Now I was seeing the person she was instead of the person she wanted me to see.

"What future do you see with Tyler now that Tiffany isn't standing in the way of your relationship?" I asked.

"We may be separated, but it won't be for long. I expect he'll come back, sooner than later. He's nothing without me."

It was a bold statement.

I had a bold statement of my own.

"I believe Tyler loved Tiffany, and she loved him," I said.

As the words poured out of my mouth, I questioned whether I'd pushed too far. She hadn't given me much of anything yet, and here I was burning down the one bridge I was trying to create.

Jana cocked her head to the side, giving her dog a pat as she said, "Anyone ever told you you're a bit of a jerk?"

"You wouldn't be the first."

"Didn't think so. I've been through a lot since I learned about the affair. You may consider yourself good at your job, but it's obvious you've never learned how to sympathize with the victim."

"When you say *victim*, are you referring to yourself?"

"Who else? I'm just as much a victim as Tiffany was in this situation."

Wow.

I bit my tongue, because if I said what I wanted to say, there would be no coming back from it.

"It's the truth," she continued. "I may still be breathing, and she's not, but Tyler betrayed us both."

I was beginning to understand Jana's earlier remark about how Tyler would come back to her because he couldn't live without her. In ways, they were two peas in a pod, both self-centered. Once the novelty of his affair with Tiffany wore off, would Tiffany's selfless, kindhearted demeanor have been enough for him?

I was getting nowhere, and Jana had turned every question I'd asked into a combative, self-serving argument. I decided my energy would be better spent elsewhere, and I'd be better off trying again another day.

"There are levels to being a victim. The fact is, *you're* still alive. *She* isn't. Think about that for a minute. And hey," I said as I stood, slinging my handbag over my shoulder, "if you consider yourself a victim, then what am I? And what kind of friend would I be if I didn't do what I'm doing now, everything in my power to solve her murder? Wouldn't you want a friend like that in your corner, someone who stood up, making sure you got the justice you deserved? I would thank you for your time, but all you've done is waste it. I'm out of here."

"Wait, I didn't mean to—"

"I no longer care what you meant or didn't mean. I'm tired of everyone running me in circles today when all I'm trying to do is get justice for my friend, the *real* victim in this situation. She didn't deserve any of this, and she didn't deserve to die."

Rant over, I bolted off the porch toward my car, coming to

an abrupt halt when she shouted, "I liked Tiffany, you know. I saw what he saw in her. She had soft edges and a tender way about her, something I know I lack."

"You don't know the first thing about her. Don't pretend like you do."

"I may have only met her once, but she drew me in from the start. I went to her office that day thinking I was going to unleash on her, maybe even smack her around a little. Within the first minute, she defused the bomb that is me—and the havoc I wreak when things don't go my way. Takes a certain kind of person to do that, a special person, and I'm sorry you lost her in the way you did."

Part of me wanted to give her the middle finger and get out of there.

Then I thought, *she could have let me leave without saying a thing.*

So why had she?

Turning to face her, I said, "Tiffany was one of the good ones. All she wanted in life was to find someone she could be happy with, and that happiness was taken from her before she even got the chance to find it."

We locked eyes, and she said, "Hey, don't leave yet. Can you wait there for just a moment?"

"Why?"

"It will all make sense if you can just give me a minute. I'll be right back."

Jana scooped up the dog and disappeared into the house. Walking toward me a minute later, she shoved a manila envelope in my hand.

"What is this?" I asked.

"When you got here, you asked me how I knew Tyler was having an affair. I was being honest when I said no one told me ... well, not in the traditional sense."

"Then how did you know about it?"

"I came out of the hair salon one day, and this envelope was beneath one of the windshield wipers on my car."

I glanced at the envelope, then back at her, narrowing my gaze. "You didn't seem interested in helping me before. In fact, you did the opposite. What changed?"

"I don't have a friend like you, someone who would go to the lengths you have for Tiffany. No matter how I feel about being dragged into the middle of this mess, I believed Tiffany when she told me she didn't know Tyler was married. And ... well, I want you to find the person who killed her. Not just for her, but for you too, because I get the sense you'll never be able to move on until you do."

18

I was sitting on Tiffany's front porch staring at the envelope in my hand. I hadn't opened it yet, and I wasn't sure why I was hesitating. If this were any other case, once it got into my hot little hands, I would have torn it open the first chance I got.

This was different somehow.

Not knowing what the contents inside might contain, I was nervous—and I liked to think I didn't get nervous. It's what I told myself, at least.

It's not going to open itself, Gigi.

Just do it.

I heeded the pep talk I'd just given myself, putting on a pair of gloves. Then I undid the clasp, pulling the flap open. Reaching in, I grabbed the contents, pulled them out, and set them on my lap, my eyes coming to rest on a series of photos—lots of photos—printed out on plain white printer paper, from the looks of it.

In one, Tiffany and Tyler were leaning against her car, embraced in a hug. In another, Tiffany, Tyler, and Ron were sitting at the table inside Tiffany's house having dinner. In yet another, the two were on the front porch, kissing.

The photos revealed patterns.

In each of them, Tiffany looked happy and content, like love had found its way to her door at long last. It was also obvious the photos had been snapped over a series of days as evidenced by the fact that Tiffany's hair and wardrobe were different in several of the images.

The one constant was the vantage point from which the photos had been taken—from outside Tiffany's house. It made sense that she and Tyler always got together at her place, given he was married and lived forty minutes away in San Luis Obispo. I bet he thought forty minutes was far enough away for him to keep his secret until he decided to let it out.

If true, I wondered whether Tiffany ever questioned why he always came to her house, or why she was never invited to his. Maybe she had questioned him. If so, what excuse would he have given? If I had been in her situation, it would have been one of the first things I asked. In that way, we were total opposites—Tiffany always trusting, and me, always questioning.

"Hello, dear."

Startled to realize I was no longer alone, I looked up. A much older woman stood in front of me, her hands on hips, her short, curly, white hair radiating in the sunlight.

I flipped the photos over, stripped off the gloves on my hands, and slid the photos back into the envelope.

"I don't believe we've met," I said.

"We haven't. I'm Queenie Jenkins. I live across the street. Who might you be?"

"Georgiana Germaine."

"Aha, the detective I've been hearing about. We've been expecting you. The neighborhood has been all abuzz about Tiffany's famous detective friend."

"I am a detective, and I was Tiffany's friend, but famous? I don't know about that."

"I do. Tiffany told Martha all about you, and Martha told Janice, and Janice told me. You're good at solving murders."

I nodded, and she smacked my shoulder.

"See there, you're just being modest," she said. "No need, not around us."

"*Us?*"

Queenie turned and shouted toward the hedges on the neighboring property. "Martha, Janice, I've made the introductions. You can come on over."

Two more women similar in age to Queenie popped their heads up and gave me a wave. They scurried over, smiling but saying nothing.

"Why were you hiding?" I asked. "You could have just come over and introduced yourself like Queenie just did."

Queenie swished a hand through the air. "Oh, Janice and Martha are both on the shy side, and we've been debating whether you wanted to be approached or not. We've been watching you through Janice's window for some time. You seem ... well, sad, if you don't mind me saying so. Not that we blame you. It's dreadful, what happened to Tiffany. We're all so sorry she's no longer with us, sorry to lose such a wonderful woman, and sorry for your loss. I realize my words of support can't fix what's happened, but we wanted to give our condolences all the same."

"I appreciate it."

It was clear Queenie was the ringleader of the group, the other two nodding as if content to let her continue to do all the talking.

"I heard Tiffany was just about to fly off to your wedding on the day she died," Queenie said.

"You heard right."

"Shame. She was looking forward to it." She turned her attention from me to the envelope in my lap. "What have you got there?"

"Photos."

"Photographic evidence, you mean?"

"I do."

All three ladies leaned in as if waiting for me to share some juicy details. When I didn't, their disappointment showed.

"How well did you all know Tiffany?" I asked.

"Martha knew her best," Queenie said. "Tiffany worked late most days. Martha often made an extra dinner plate for her and would take it to her when she pulled into the driveaway ... on the nights she was alone, of course."

Turning toward Martha, Queenie said, "Go on, Martha. Tell her about your friendship with Tiffany."

Martha appeared nervous to be put on the spot, but she took a deep breath and began. "I spoke to her often, and I knew a good deal about her life, like the new beau she was seeing. Well, he wasn't new, I suppose. They'd been dating several months."

"Are you talking about Tyler?"

"The very same," Queenie said.

"Did any of you ever meet or talk with him?" I asked.

"I wouldn't say he was the talking sort. They took walks together sometimes, and whenever Tiffany would stop to say hello it was as if he was in a rush for the conversation to be over. Odd fellow, if you ask me. Not like the other fellow."

"What *other* fellow?"

Queenie pressed a finger to her lips. "There was a man who came around before Tiffany started seeing Tyler. She never introduced him to any of us, but we chatted with him a few times. He was so nice, always smiling and giving us a friendly wave."

"Did Tiffany ever talk to you about the other guy?"

"She did not, even though we pushed her for details, asking her who he was and if they were dating."

"What did she say?"

"She described the man as being a friend. He was not just a friend, though. Not a chance. I saw them cuddled up on the couch on multiple occasions."

"He also spent the night," Martha added. "I saw him leave one morning when I was out watering my flowers."

"How long was Tiffany seeing the other guy before she started dating Tyler?"

Queenie turned toward Janice. "You should take this one, Janice. You're the numbers gal in the group."

"Let's see now," Janice said. "Forty-six days."

I was shocked at her precision.

"Forty-six days?" I asked.

"Correct. She was first seen with the other man forty-six days before she started seeing Tyler. I saw them together fourteen … no, fifteen times."

"During what time period?"

"Two months before Tyler started coming around."

It seemed bizarre to me that they had such detailed information, though I was glad to have it. I imagined they were all retired with nothing better to do than stay up to date on every little happening in the neighborhood.

Still, I questioned *how* they knew so much.

"You three seem to have a lot of details about Tiffany's life," I said. "More than the usual neighbor would have about someone. Is there anything else you need to tell me?"

19

Queenie reached inside her bag, pulling out a pair of binoculars and holding them up with pride. "Now, before you say anything, I'm well aware that we've been a bit nosy, involving ourselves in Tiffany's private moments here and there," she said. "We were just looking out for her interests, you see. Forgive me for speaking ill of the dead, but she struck me as the kind of person who needed a little looking after."

"I'm not here to judge you."

"It's not just Tiffany," Janice said. "People around the neighborhood call us the Granny Guard. Not much gets past us … well, except Tiffany's murder, of course. We've been beside ourselves because we weren't around when it happened."

"We were at the market that day," Queenie said. "Terrible timing. Seems ballsy to murder someone in the middle of the day."

Tiffany's backyard opened to a wooded area, lush with trees, the perfect way to sneak in and out of her place without being seen, which explained why the killer may have been so brazen.

"Did any of you see anything suspicious around the time of Tiffany's murder, or in the weeks or months before it?" I asked.

"One strange thing, yes," Queenie said. "One night I saw a man one snapping pictures of Tiffany and her beau through her living room window."

"How long ago?"

"Been at least a couple of months now, maybe even longer. I tried to speak to him, but when he saw me coming his way, he took off."

"Did you get a good look at him?"

"It was dark out, and he had a ballcap on. Kept his head down when he zoomed past me in a black truck. Sorry to say I couldn't make out the license plate. My eyes these days ... I'm afraid I don't see so well anymore."

I turned my thoughts back to the other mystery man. I wondered who he was and if he could be involved in Tiffany's murder. She didn't always mention the new men in her life to me right away. Still, it bugged me that I didn't know about him.

"The other man," I said, "the one Tiffany dated before Tyler ... what did he look like?"

"He was a real looker," Queenie said.

"Oh, yes," Janice added. "Handsome, like a young Orson Welles, and just as tall. Broad shoulders, dark, wavy hair."

"We were excited about him," Queenie said.

"Why?"

"He had kind eyes, and the way he looked at her ... it was so sweet."

Tall, handsome, broad shoulders, and dark, wavy hair.

Orson Welles adjacent.

I knew one man who fit that description—Furniture Salesman Chad.

If I was right, and they'd started dating again, I knew why she hadn't told me. I didn't approve of him the first time they'd dated. He was nice enough, but he had no plans for his future, no ambition. He liked being a furniture salesman and had no desire to make anything more of himself.

Once, when the three of us were sitting around Tiffany's table playing cards, he told me he worked to live, unlike most Americans who, according to him, lived to work.

At the time, I couldn't relate to his way of thinking.

I, myself, was always looking to the future, to the next challenge in life, opportunities to push myself that I hadn't tried yet. So, when she asked me what I thought of Chad, I told her.

Thinking back on it now, I realized I'd been seeing him from my perspective, holding him to my standards, not hers. She didn't care about his lack of ambition. She had enough of it for them both. If I had to do it all over again, I would have been more supportive, focusing on what she wanted than what I wanted for her.

"If I may be candid," Martha said. "I always thought there was something shady about Tyler, even though Tiffany gushed about him."

"She wasn't always the smartest cookie when it came to choosing suitors," Queenie added. "Are the rumors true? Is Tyler a married man?"

"The rumors are true."

"What a pity."

"Did you ever see him arguing or behaving in a negative way toward her?"

In unison, they shook their heads.

"While he gave off an unsavory vibe, they did seem happy when they were together, always smiling and laughing," Queenie said. "But if he was hiding a wife, I call everything about him into question. Do you think he murdered her?"

"I don't know."

"I expect you've spoken to him by now, hmmm?"

"I talked to him this morning."

Queenie moved a hand to her hip. "Well, what did you think?"

"It's too early to tell."

"You look like someone who cares a great deal about first impressions. You must have some inclination about the man."

Most of the time when I was questioned in the way I was now, I looked for ways to dodge them. But these women were watchers. They saw things, heard things, kept their ears to the ground, and I suspected, in everyone else's business. Having them as allies made sense.

Perhaps I had more to learn from them than they had to learn from me.

With that in mind, I decided I'd share more than usual.

"This morning, I spoke to Jordan, a man Tyler works with, and then to Tyler himself. I also visited Tyler's wife, Jana. As I've thought about those conversations, I get the feeling Tyler and Jana got together after Tiffany's death to decide what they were going to say to the police."

"Why would they do that if they were innocent?" Queenie asked.

"To create a narrative, a story they'd tell me and the police, a narrative I question."

"If they're innocent, I see no reason why they'd do such a thing."

"Tyler and Jana are smart enough to know they'd both be suspects. Even if they're innocent, I can see them wanting to protect each other."

Queenie tapped her foot to the ground. "This Jana ... what does she look like?"

"Slender, early thirties, long, dark hair, hipster vibe."

"And what does she drive?"

"There was a blue sedan parked in the driveway when I arrived at her house. I assumed it was hers."

As soon as I'd delivered the information, all three women huddled up like they were deliberating a play on a football field. I leaned in, trying to hear what they were saying but only made out bits and pieces. No sooner had they gathered, they broke from the huddle, turning toward me.

"We believe we've seen her," Queenie said.

"We sure do," Martha added.

"When ... and where?" I asked.

"Parked across the street from Tiffany's house, not two weeks ago. She was in a bright blue sedan. Stood out like spring in the dead of winter."

"What was she doing there, do you know?"

"Similar to what the other man was doing. She was crouched down in the driver's seat, watching Tyler and Tiffany through the living room window."

"She watched them for forty-seven minutes," Janice said.

"Did she ever get out of the car, or approach Tiffany's house, or anything else?"

"She stayed in the car the entire time," Martha said.

"That's when we first thought Tyler was double-dipping," Queenie said.

"Oh, yes," Janice added. "Double-dipping, to be sure."

"Double-dipping?" I asked.

"Seeing two women at the same time," Janice said. "What we didn't know was if she was another girl he was dating, or if she was his wife."

"We discussed it amongst ourselves and decided I would approach her and find out," Queenie said. "I walked to the car and tapped on the window. The woman refused to put the window down. I asked if she knew Tiffany and why she was parked across from her house."

"How did she react?"

"Not well, I'm afraid. Without a single word, she started the car and took off down the road."

"Did you ever see her again?"

"We haven't, no."

"What about security cameras?" I asked. "I assume many of the residents on this street have them."

"Some do," Queenie said. "We don't."

"Why not?"

"We prefer our binoculars."

Old school. I wasn't surprised.

"Is there anything else I should know?" I asked.

They looked at one another and shook their heads. "Not that we can think of right now."

I reached into my bag, pulling out a few business cards and handing them out. "Here's my contact information. If you can think of anything else, or if you see or hear anything suspicious, give me a call."

20

"I was wondering when I'd see you," Chad said. "It's been a while."

He'd aged well since the last time I saw him, looking a lot more muscular and well-dressed than I remembered. As I looked him over, I noticed a gash on his right hand, and I wondered how he got it.

"I was just at Tiffany's house," I said, "and a few of the older women who live on the same street described a man who was dating Tiffany several months ago. The man they described reminded me of you."

"Uh, yeah, it was me. Tiffany didn't tell you?"

"She didn't, and I'm trying to figure out why."

Chad glanced around the furniture showroom, lowering his voice. "Can we talk somewhere else?"

"Sure, when do you get off work?"

"Not for another four hours. I haven't taken my break yet today, though. Let me speak to the manager. I'll meet you out front in a few minutes."

I nodded and walked to my car, leaning against it as I waited.

Six minutes later, Chad exited the store, his hands shoved into his pockets as he approached me. "I have fifteen minutes."

"Not a long break."

"We're short-staffed today. I was lucky to get anything."

"You have a sizable cut on your hand. What happened?"

"I was in a hurry the other day when I was opening boxes in the back room of the store, and ... well, I lost a fight with a boxcutter."

It seemed like a logical explanation.

But was it?

"I saw a wall of plaques when I entered the store," I said. "You're the employee of the month. Well done."

He looked down, sighing as he kicked a few pebbles around. "You don't have to be polite, and you don't have to pretend, not with me."

"The compliment was genuine."

"I know you've never approved of me. And hey, I get it. You wanted the best for Tiffany, and in your mind, I wasn't it."

"What makes you think I didn't approve? Did Tiffany say something to you?"

"I never knew all her reasons for breaking up with me the first time," he said. "When we met up again, she admitted you felt she could do a lot better than me."

It was something I'd said in confidence—girl talk. Or so I thought.

"I never knew she'd said anything to you," I said. "How could I? She didn't even tell me you'd started dating again."

"She didn't want to keep it from you, and just so you know, I advised her to tell you."

"Why?"

"She felt bad keeping it a secret."

I wished she had felt confident enough to tell me.

My advice, had she asked for it a second time, may have been a lot different.

"When did you start dating again, and which one of you reached out first?" I asked.

"About nine months ago, I pulled into a gas station, and there she was, standing out front, sipping on a giant, blue slushy drink. We made eye contact, and the next thing I knew, we'd decided to go for a drive. It ended up being one of the best, most honest conversations we'd ever had."

"What did you talk about?"

He crossed his arms, narrowing his eyes. "Are you sure you want to know?"

"I do."

"She said she'd been under a lot of stress the first time we dated. She was still getting over the last guy. She wasn't in the right headspace to give our relationship what it needed to thrive. That was part of the reason she called it quits."

"And the other part?"

He looked away, going quiet, giving me an idea of the "other part,"—*me*.

"You're the other part," he said. "You told her you thought she was better off with someone who was goal-driven and motivated, like her."

Hearing my words coming back at me, I felt awful about having said them. But I deserved to hear it.

"Tiffany asked me for my honest opinion," I said. "Some things I mentioned were favorable, and others were not. I never suggested she should break up with you."

"I don't think you realize just how much she looked up to you. Your approval meant everything."

"Tiffany didn't need my approval, and she knew it. She was the best of us, a much better person than I'll ever be. Look, I'm sorry."

"Is that why you came here, to apologize? I don't need your apology. We've both just lost someone who meant a lot to each of us, and I'd rather not stand here reminiscing."

Talking with him now, I had such a different impression of him than I had before. He was mature and well-spoken. I supposed I'd missed it because I'd never spent much time with him. In fact, this was the first one-on-one conversation we'd ever had.

"What happened after the night you reconnected at the gas station?" I asked.

"I asked if she was single. She said yes, and I asked her on a date. She didn't commit at first. About a week later, after a bad day at work, she texted me and invited me over."

"Did she tell you what happened at work that day?"

"She'd taken on a big divorce case and was doing everything in her power to ensure her client, the soon-to-be ex-wife, got everything she deserved in the divorce settlement. The husband's lawyers were relentless, coming at Tiffany with everything they had. It was a lot of pressure, and she was struggling to deal with it."

I remembered the case.

The husband was worth billions.

He'd hired not one, not two, but three lawyers, which may have had something to do with the multiple affairs he'd had during the marriage.

"She worked with her colleague, Everett, on that case," I said. "And they won it, just a few weeks ago. I'd never seen her more relieved to be finished with a case in her life."

He crossed his arms. "She was relieved, at first, until her client's husband cornered her as they were both leaving the gym. He threatened to ruin her life because she'd ruined his."

"Tiffany told me they'd had a run-in, but I didn't know he threatened her. Did he follow up on the threat in any way?"

"I don't know. To be honest, I hadn't heard much from her after we broke up the second time."

"Then how do you know about her run-in with the husband?"

"She texted me and told me about it. Then she apologized for texting me and said she shouldn't have because she was in a relationship with someone else."

I found it curious that she'd texted him.

At the same time, Chad had a softness about him. After their first breakup, Tiffany described him as the one guy you knew you could always lean on, telling your deepest, darkest secrets to, and he would never paint you in a negative light. I figured it was the reason she'd given him another shot.

"Tell me about the second time you dated," I said.

"After we got together at her house, we saw each other almost every day for a while. I'd almost forgotten how intoxicating she could be—her laugh, her positivity, her love of life."

"Her laugh was timeless. I can still hear it."

"Me, too. When I was given a second chance, I spent a lot of time in those first several weeks thinking about why things hadn't worked out the first time. I was determined to make sure it didn't happen again."

"I wish I would have known."

He let out a short, dry laugh—more scoff than amusement —dripping with sarcasm as he shook his head. "I don't."

"No, you don't understand. My advice would have been different. It's just, when you dated the first time, I was going through a lot in my life. It's possible I projected some of my feelings onto her, even though I was unaware I was doing it back then. I see that now. All I would have wanted was her happiness."

He nodded, and I hoped he believed me.

"Tiffany told me you lost your daughter, and then you quit your job, split from your husband, and left town," he said. "You went through a lot, and I'm sure she told you, but she was so proud of you."

I stared down at my hands.

They were clenched into tight fists, pushing down the emotions creeping up inside me.

"I can't imagine why she was proud of me," I said. "I was a tornado in heels."

"You may have seen yourself that way, but she saw a woman who pushed through her past, got her life back together, and started dating a man she'd cared for since college."

"We just got married."

"I'm happy for you."

And I was sad for him.

It was obvious how much he cared for Tiffany, and how hopeful he had been for a life they would never have.

"Why didn't it work the second time?" I asked.

"*He* showed up."

"Tyler?"

"Yep, the guy ruined everything. One minute we were fine; the next, she was questioning our future again. The breakup was hard the first time. The second ... well, I suppose I felt the same way you did, a tornado in tennis shoes."

He was pained.

I could see it on his face.

Talking about her was difficult for him, even now.

Chad didn't seem like the murdering type, but it didn't mean he wasn't.

"How did the relationship end?" I asked.

"She told me she'd started having feelings for her realtor,

feelings she wanted to explore, and she thought it was best to be honest with me about it. I tried to fight for what we were rebuilding, but once he entered the picture, I didn't stand a chance."

"Whenever Tiffany told me about a new man in her life, I always did my homework," I said.

"Oh, I know."

"With Tyler, I was in full wedding-planning mode, and I'm sorry to say, I didn't look into him. If I had, I would have found out he was married."

Chad let out a long, frustrated sigh. "He's *married*?"

"Yeah, and maybe if I had known, if I had told her, I could have saved her life somehow."

"You can't say that."

"I just did. I've spent the last few days treating myself like an emotional punching bag. She needed me, and I wasn't there."

"What happened isn't your fault."

I knew that, and yet, no matter how many times someone said it to me, I couldn't shake the feeling.

He glanced at the cell phone in his hand, checking the time. "I need to go in a minute."

"I understand. Aside from the message Tiffany sent, telling you about the confrontation with her client's husband, did you ever hear from her again?"

"No, but in that same message, she was full of apologies for shutting me out of her life like she did."

A short, middle-aged woman pushed the store door open and tipped her head toward Chad. "We need ya back on the floor."

"Be right there," he said.

She nodded and slid back inside.

Chad started for the door, then turned. "You're not the only one carrying around guilt. Hearing from her that night just added to the pain I was already going through, so I decided to block her number. I'll regret that for the rest of my life."

<h1 style="text-align:center">21</h1>

I was sitting on a chair on my back balcony, sipping on a glass of prosecco as I talked with Foley and Whitlock about my day. Draped over my feet was Luka, who seemed happy and content to have me home.

"You've been busy today," Foley said.

"So have the two of you," I replied. "And from the sounds of it, we talked to a few of the same people. How are we feeling about Jordan, Tyler, and Jana?"

Whitlock glanced at Foley and then at me. "I think there's something to your suspicion that the husband and wife got together after Tiffany was murdered to discuss what they were going to say to us. Seems a bit strange though, *if* they're innocent."

"Jana knew it wouldn't take long for us to find out about Tyler's indiscretion and consider him a suspect," I said. "And Tyler strikes me as the kind of person who blurts things out when he's cornered, says things he maybe shouldn't say but does anyway. Jana must know this about him, so I can see her talking to him about what he'd say when he was questioned."

"After what he did, I'm surprised she's considering taking him back," Whitlock said.

"I'm a little surprised too. She comes across as tough and confident—someone who doesn't take any nonsense—but maybe it's all a façade."

Foley shrugged. "Maybe."

"We can all agree they're still suspects," I said. "On another note, what did you think of Tiffany's neighbors, the older ladies?"

"They're a funny bunch," Whitlock said. "I found them to be enjoyable. If we wouldn't have had other places to be, I could have talked to those gals for hours."

With a subtle lift of his brow, Foley made his disapproval known. "Not sure I found them as witty as you did. *Meddling* seems like a more appropriate word."

"They may meddle, but they sure know a lot," I said. "Did they talk to you about the other guy Tiffany was seeing, the one before Tyler?"

"They did not."

"As soon as they described him to me, I knew they were talking about Chad. He's a salesman at Willow Roost, a furniture store in San Luis Obispo. Tiffany had dated him once before. I talked to him today, and he told me they started up a second time ... before Tiffany met Tyler."

"What's the skinny on the guy?" Whitlock asked. "Fun fact, which is unrelated but fun, the term 'the skinny' was American military slang originating in the '40s, during World War II. It means 'What's the news,' or 'What's the information,' or in today's slang, 'Spill the beans.'"

And I had plenty of beans to spill.

"Tiffany never told me about dating Chad a second time."

Foley leaned back, adjusting his tie. "Why wouldn't she?"

"I didn't approve of him the first time they dated, and I

guess she decided to hold off on saying anything when they picked back up again."

"Why didn't you approve?"

I took another sip of my prosecco, setting the glass down as I prepared my confession. "I thought Chad wasn't good enough for her. I may have been wrong about that, and I've been dwelling on it all evening."

"Aww, I wouldn't be too hard on yourself," Foley said. "She was a big girl. She made her own decisions. What else can you tell us about round two with Chad?"

"Chad thought things were going well the second time around, and then she met Tyler, and she ... well, dropped him to pursue Tyler."

Foley slapped his knee. "Sounds like motive for murder to me. What's your take on the guy?"

"He admitted the breakup was harder on him the second time than the first. And sure, he had motive. I'm just not sure he has the temperament to commit murder, though. He seems too soft."

"So did Jeffrey Dahmer. People described him as quiet and polite. And yeah, the guy was socially awkward, so much so that people didn't see him as threatening."

"And then when that kid escaped in '91, cops found out Dahmer had murdered seventeen people," Whitlock added.

I sighed. "I get it. I didn't say I'd ruled him out yet. The fact is, we have several people to focus on right now."

"We weren't trying to give you a hard time," Whitlock said.

"I know."

Foley's cell phone buzzed. He pulled it from his pocket and turned toward us, saying, "Be right back."

He went inside the house, returning less than a minute later.

"That was fast," I said.

"It was your sister, Phoebe. I'm late for dinner."

"I'm sure she understands."

"Of course she does. She's far more understanding than she should be. Still, we should wrap up and reconvene later."

"Before you go, there's something I haven't mentioned yet, or rather, someone. I'll be right back."

I walked to my bedroom, lifted my handbag off the doorknob, and met them both in the kitchen. I placed the bag on the counter, pulling out the envelope inside.

"What do you have there?" Foley asked.

"It just might be the best piece of information I've received all day. When I visited Jana, she was standoffish at first, but by the end of our conversation, she came around. I asked her how she knew about Tyler's affair. Turns out, someone left this envelope under one of her windshield wipers."

"What's in the envelope?" Whitlock asked.

"Photos of Tiffany and Tyler—photos proving he was having an affair."

"Any idea who left them on her car?"

"Queenie said she saw a man taking photos of the two of them across the street from Tiffany's house one night," I said. "He drove a black truck. She didn't get a good look at him."

"It's a start," Foley said.

"Also, in terms of suspects, there was a divorce case Tiffany was working on several months ago that just wrapped up a few weeks ago. I remember the case. We talked about it a few times. It was hard on her, but she did end up winning the case. Her client's husband didn't take the loss well. According to Chad, he confronted Tiffany and threatened to ruin her life."

Foley and Whitlock nodded, exchanging worrisome glances.

"How long ago?" Foley asked.

"It was after the case came to an end, so it hasn't been long.

It's something to consider, though. If this disgruntled man wanted payback, a good place to start is by alerting Jana to the fact her husband was cheating. It would have blown up Tiffany's world, to find out the man she knew and loved had been lying to her all along."

"Do you have a name?"

"I will tomorrow. Once you've looked them over, will you pass them on to Silas?"

Foley reached for the envelope and nodded. "I will, though I'm not sure what kind of forensic magic Silas can glean from them."

"He can lift prints, if there are any. Several years back, before you were the chief of police, and I was still a detective working for the department, Silas worked a case where he managed to lift a partial off an envelope."

Paper was delicate to work with, but it could be done. The best way was with ninhydrin, which reacts with amino acids in the fingerprint residue, producing a purplish-blue print, called Ruhemann's purple. Then it's sprayed or brushed on the paper. After the paper dries, heat is applied. If there are viable fingerprints, ones that aren't smeared or too small to make out, Silas would be able to see them as soon as a few hours following treatment.

"You said 'as soon as ...' I'm assuming it could take longer?"

"It could take a few days. I don't even know if it will work. There are other ways he can test too. If he goes with the ninhydrin method, the paper can't be reused for other tests. The good thing is, we have several pictures to test."

"You're saying he can test them in a variety of ways, right?" Whitlock asked.

"He can, and knowing Silas, he will. Give him the photos. He'll know what to do."

22

I entered 2 Little Figs, my favorite local coffee shop the following morning, and I glanced around. My eyes came to rest on a man dressed in a fitted olive-colored suit and black pinstriped tie. We made eye contact, and he nodded, offering a slight smile, as I walked over, sitting across from him in the booth.

"Hello, Everett."

He rubbed his temples as if trying to press the negative thoughts away. "It's good to see you, Georgiana, though I'd prefer it if it were under different circumstances."

"I would too. How have you been?"

It was a stupid question.

I *knew* how he was doing.

I guessed the same as me.

"I've been better," he said. "You?"

"Trying to live with the reality of what's happened, though I suspect it would be a whole lot easier to live in denial."

"Tell me about it. I can't believe it, you know? I just saw Tiffany a week ago. We had a nice chat, caught up on both of our lives. She wasn't in the best of spirits that day, but she was excited for your wedding. I'm assuming it was a joyous occasion?"

"It was, although the moment I heard about what happened to Tiffany, everything changed," I said. "All I wanted was to get back here and nail the guy who did this to her. A few of the wedding guests knew what happened to Tiffany on the day of my wedding, but they waited until the next morning to tell me. I think I knew before that, though. I had a strange dream that night."

"I've been having strange dreams too."

If he only knew ...

"In the past week, I've learned some things Tiffany never mentioned to me," I said.

He tapped a finger to the table, nodding. "Before we get too far into this conversation, I'm in desperate need of a cup of coffee."

I scooted out of the booth. "I'll get you one. How do you take it?"

"Black, no sugar."

"Coming right up."

As I walked to the front counter, my thoughts were on Everett. While he looked polished and presentable on the outside, I imagined he was scarred on the inside, just like me. Everett hadn't just been Tiffany's work colleague; he'd been her closest guy friend for over twenty years. They first met in law school and had even tried dating each other at one time. It wasn't long before they realized that although they shared a great affection for one another, they were better friends than they were lovers.

If anyone knew about the things Tiffany hadn't told me, it was him. Not only had he worked with her day in and day out, but I'd also always found him to be a perfect listener, offering unwavering support. He was a lot like Tiffany in that way.

I ordered Everett a coffee, a lavender, oat-milk latte for myself, and a couple of cheese Danishes, because … well, anything that included cheese in its name was hard to resist, wasn't it?

As I returned to the table, I glanced out the window, noticing a green vintage sedan parked across the street under a shade tree. It had been idling there since I'd pulled into the parking lot, idling. Maybe nothing of note, but I was sure I'd seen that exact car on Tiffany's street yesterday.

I sat my offerings on the table and said, "I'm sure you know why I asked to see you this morning. If it's too hard to talk here, we can go somewhere else—somewhere we're not overheard as much as we might if we stay here."

"Where do you suggest?"

"We could take a stroll around the park. It's often quiet in the morning and not too busy. And given we can walk from here; it seems like a good option."

He agreed, and we gathered up our items, exiting the coffee shop. As we crossed the street, I turned my attention back to the idling car and the lady I could see slouching in the driver's seat.

I turned toward Everett, saying. "I think I'm being followed."

"Oh?"

I tipped my head toward the car. "I met a few older ladies yesterday, inquisitive, boundary-pushing types. It seems one of them, the ringleader of the group, is tracking my every move now. I should go and talk with her. You're welcome to come with me, if you'd like."

"Sure, why not?"

We changed course, heading straight for the sedan. The moment its occupant spotted me, she attempted to lower herself even farther into the seat, but it was far too late.

She'd been made.

I tapped a knuckle to the glass. "Open up, Queenie. There's no use hiding. I know you've been following me."

She sat straight up, smiling as the window came down.

"Why hello, Detective," she said. "Fancy meeting you here. I've been out running a few early morning errands."

"Errands that include following me around town?"

"Oh, no. I've done nothing of the kind. In fact, I was just thinking of getting myself a cup of tea, and since 2 Little Figs has so many options ... well, here I am."

I crossed my arms. "It doesn't take ten minutes to get out of the car and walk over. If you planned on getting a cup of tea, why are you still sitting here?"

"How do you know how long I've been here?"

"I saw you out the window of the café."

Queenie pressed her wrists together and extended them toward me, tossing her head back as she snorted a laugh. "Well, I suppose the jig is up. Go ahead, arrest me for being at the same place at the same time as you."

"It's not funny."

She waved me off, shifting her attention to Everett. "And who might you be, handsome?"

I turned toward Everett, head shaking. "You don't need to answer."

"It's all right. I'm Everett."

"What are you doing here, Queenie?" I asked.

"Helping you with your case, of course."

"How is *following me* helping?"

"I don't know how many times I have to say I *wasn't* following you, though I'm glad I ran into you. I tried calling. You didn't answer."

"When?"

"This morning."

I picked my phone out of my pocket and looked at it,

shocked to see I'd had two missed calls from the same unknown number. In my haste to get to the coffee shop on time, I'd forgotten to turn the ringer back on.

"My ringer was on silent," I said. "Why did you call?"

"I saw someone," Queenie said, "inside Tiffany's house—a man, not one hour ago."

"How do you know it was a man and not a woman?"

"He was tall."

"Women can be tall too, you know. Did you get a look at his face?"

"I did not."

"Where is he now?"

"He left in a white pickup truck. I have the license plate written down in my notebook, but we won't be needing it now *will we*, Mr. Everett?"

It seemed she wasn't following me, after all.

She was following *him*, and I was sure she was shocked to arrive at the coffee shop to find the two of us together.

I turned to Everett, whose face had gone pale. "Well? Were you at Tiffany's house this morning?"

"I can explain," he said.

"Good. I can't wait to hear it."

"I was there, yes. But I didn't break in. I have a key."

"Why?" I asked.

"After your wedding, Tiffany planned to stay in New York for a couple of weeks."

"I had no idea. She never told me."

"She thought a little time away might help her clear her head and move past the breakup."

"Sounds like something she would do, though it doesn't explain why you have a key to her house or why you were there this morning."

Queenie shifted positions, leaning closer.

"I planned on telling you as soon as we got to the park," he said. "I was there to water the plants."

Queenie wagged a disapproving finger in his direction. "No offense, but I find it curious why she asked *you* to do it when she could have asked one of her neighbors."

"They're good friends," I said.

"If they were such good friends, why did he leave her house with a piece of paper in his hand, eh?"

I had to say, I was impressed with her questions.

"A couple of weeks ago, we took on a new client," Everett said. "We were supposed to meet with them, but after what happened to Tiffany, I took some days off. This morning the client pressed me to have the meeting, and I realized I was missing the last page of their signed agreement."

"How did you know you'd find it at Tiffany's house?"

"She'd taken the file home to look it over a few days before she died, and she'd made me a copy. I hadn't noticed the missing page until this morning. I went to the house, watered the plants, and looked around for it."

"Why bother watering the plants now that she's dead?"

"I ... ahh, the plant in the living room has sentimental meaning. I bought it for her as a housewarming gift. I thought I'd water it, then talk to you to see when you thought I could take it from her house."

"I don't understand how the missing page just happened to be there," I said. "The police did a full sweep of her place. Wouldn't they have found it and taken it in with the rest of the evidence?"

"I found the missing page on the scanner, and since the lid was closed, I'm guessing she forgot to take it out, and they didn't look under there."

It made sense, though I was still on the suspicious side.

But Everett was one of the best people I knew, and I didn't take him for a liar.

"You're not supposed to enter a house that's an active crime scene until it's been cleared," I said.

"There was no crime scene tape up. I thought it would be okay. I have the paper I took in my car. I can show it to you if you want."

I shook my head. "There's no need. I believe you."

"I don't," Queenie said. "I've seen just about everyone who's been in and out of her home. If you're such a good friend, why haven't I seen *you* before?"

"We're together all day at work," he said. "And I have a family—a wife, and two kids. If we needed to talk about work stuff after hours, we called or texted each other."

Queenie looked at me. "What do we think? Is Mr. Everett here telling the truth?"

"My last name's Whittaker."

"Shush, young man. I wasn't speaking to you, now was I?"

"I've known him a long time," I said. "I believe he's telling the truth. I appreciate the fact you're keeping an eye out, Queenie. But, please, stop following people. I can take it from here."

23

With Queenie gone, Everett and I finished our drinks and Danishes and took a stroll around the park.

"You were right about her being an inquisitive, boundary-pushing type," Everett said. "That Queenie, she's intense."

"She's a lot to take in," I said. "When she and her two friends approached me when I was at Tiffany's house yesterday, I wasn't planning on talking to them for as long as I did. The longer we talked, the more I realized how much they knew about Tiffany's life—things I didn't even know."

"Like what?"

"Before Tiffany met Tyler, she'd started dating Chad again. Did you know?"

"Yeah, and I'm sorry she kept it from you."

"Don't be. It's not your fault. It's not even hers. It's mine. I wasn't his biggest fan. I'm guessing she didn't tell me because she didn't think I'd approve of them getting back together."

"She didn't plan on keeping it from you for long. She wanted to make sure dating him again was the right decision."

"Why did she decide to give him another chance?"

He gave the question some thought. "In my opinion, she was tired of going home to an empty house every night. We were talking once, and she said she was at the point in her life where she'd come to terms with never finding her one true love. Chad had always treated her right, so when they happened upon each other, she convinced herself she could love him enough to make it work."

It was hard to hear.

Here I was living a life of bliss with Giovanni, not knowing she'd started to believe a love like that was something she'd never have.

"It sounds like you're saying she thought about settling for Chad," I said.

Everett fidgeted with the cuff of his sleeve, gazing in the opposite direction. "Yeah, 'settling' … that's a good way to put it."

"I can understand her reasoning. When my daughter died, and I removed myself from society, being out there, alone in a camper in the woods for so long, it was the worst time of my life. There were days when I was so desperate for human inter-action, I considered returning to town and finding someone I could live with—someone who may not have been a great match but was 'good enough.'"

"Why wouldn't you have tried for a great match, if you don't mind me asking?"

"I didn't think I had a lot to offer someone at that time. Then Giovanni stepped back into my life again, and it was like I'd been given a second chance."

"I've been with my wife, Beth, since high school. The first time we met, I knew she was everything I'd always wanted."

"I feel the same way about Giovanni. There have been many times where I think back to that time of isolation and how I had thought about settling. It wasn't a good idea, and I realize that now. Perhaps Tiffany realized it too, and that's what led to the implosion of Tiffany and Chad."

"The Tyler implosion."

We passed a cluster of trees with a rustic wooden park bench in its center, and I suggested we sit for a spell, which we did.

"Have you ever met Tyler?" I asked.

"I have."

"And?"

Everett leaned back, stretching his legs. "I don't know what she saw in him. I thought he was self-absorbed and full of himself, and that was *before* I learned he was a lying, cheating dirtbag."

I'd always found Everett to be a polite, kindhearted person toward most people.

For him to say what he just had spoke volumes.

"Why do you think Tiffany was so enamored with him?" I asked.

"I don't know, maybe because he doted on her. He did a great job of making her feel seen. I can't believe I'm saying this, but even after we learned he'd cheated on his wife, as awful as it was, I still didn't doubt his affection for Tiffany. It seemed real —to me, at least."

"I heard he begged her to take him back."

"He did, and hey, she wanted to find a way to get past it, but she knew she'd never be able to trust him again. The cheating wasn't even what hurt her most."

"It was the lie itself, wasn't it?"

Everett nodded.

"When she refused to remain in the relationship, I wonder how desperate he became," I said. "Desperate enough to kill her rather than accept the fact that they were over?"

"I couldn't say. You're a better judge of character than I am."

"I'd say you're an excellent judge of character."

"Is Tyler your main suspect?"

"He's one of them."

When we'd first sat down on the bench, I was grateful for the break. Between the time we'd spent standing during our conversation with Queenie and our walk, I thought the bench would offer a nice reprieve. The longer we sat, the more the splinters in the aging planks of wood were poking me in areas I didn't like being poked.

I adjusted my position.

"I consider Tyler's wife, Jana, a suspect too," I said. "Were you there the day she showed up at the law office?"

"Yeah, I was in Tiffany's office, preparing for a meeting with a client. The next thing I know, the office door blows open, and this woman comes barging in, pointing at Tiffany and accusing her of having an affair with her husband. It was, in a word, *surreal*, like the kind of thing you hear about but don't expect to witness yourself."

"How did Tiffany react?"

"She was stunned at first. She didn't speak. She just sat there, looking at me. I'll never forget it, the look on her face."

I'd seen that look once, right after her mother died. It was like someone had reached a hand inside her soul, shattering it into a million pieces.

"When Tiffany did speak, what did she say?" I asked.

"It was Jana who spoke. She plopped down on a chair, narrowing her eyes at Tiffany like she was confused about her reaction to her accusation."

"The version of the story Tiffany's father told me was a little different."

"Tiffany may have left out of few details, but overall, what happened was true."

"What happened after Jana plopped down on the chair?"

"She seemed to realize Tiffany didn't know Tyler was married. She said, 'Wait, you didn't know, did you?'"

"What did Tiffany say?"

"She told her she didn't. I wondered if Jana thought Tiffany was lying at first. But she seemed to accept she was telling the truth, and then her entire demeanor softened. She apologized to Tiffany, saying she had a whole speech planned out, a speech meant for the woman who knew Tyler was married. Once she realized Tiffany didn't know, they had an uncomfortable but friendly chat."

"What did they talk about?"

"They discussed what should happen next. Tiffany said she would break it off that evening, and Jana asked if she could speak to Tyler first, to confront him about what he'd done and the fact both women knew about it."

"She made him dinner that night, his favorite dish, which seems like a strange thing to do," I said. "I forgot to ask her when I saw her, but after talking to her, I think I know why she did it. She wanted him to know what he'd be missing out on."

I shifted in my seat again, which didn't make anything better.

"Are you all right?" Everett asked.

"This bench is uncomfortable."

"I couldn't agree more."

"Should we finish our walk?"

He nodded, and we stood.

"I wanted to see you today to ask about the last client you and Tiffany had," I said. "I hear the husband threatened Tiffany after she won the case, for the wife."

"The client's name is Rylie Fairfax, and her husband is Landon Fairfax. I was glad you asked to meet this morning, because I've been meaning to talk to you about him. When I described Tyler as a self-absorbed person, times that by ten, and you have Landon."

"Did he threaten you too?"

"He did not."

"Why do you think he took all his rage out on her but spared you from it?"

Everett sighed, which was all the answer I needed.

"Tiffany was a woman," I said. "You're a man. I'm guessing Landon's the kind of guy who doesn't believe women are in the same playing field as men. I bet he even respected you for besting him in court. But Tiffany was different. She outsmarted him, and he couldn't let it go. Sound about right?"

"Sad to say it does."

"I heard he threatened to ruin her life."

"That's what he said, yes."

"What was her response?"

"At first, she was going to ignore him, get in her car, and leave."

"And then?"

He glanced up at the sky, shaking his head. "I ... ahh, feel strange saying it."

"Whatever it is, you can tell me."

"She told him it wasn't wise to threaten her, and then she made a threat of her own. She said she had a powerful friend with powerful connections. If he took any action against her, the life that would be ruined wouldn't be hers—it would be his."

I supposed I was a powerful friend, and Giovanni the powerful connection. I couldn't have been prouder of my friend for standing up for herself the way she had, except for one meddling thought: Had Tiffany's attempt to stand up for herself backfired, leading to her murder?

24

As I drove to my office, I thought about the conversation I'd just had with Everett. I considered the fact that Landon may have hired a private investigator to follow Tiffany around, gathering information about her private life. If so, I imagined he was pleased to know he had the upper hand at last, a way to strip away the illusion—the man she loved wasn't who he seemed.

If Landon had learned of Tyler's affair, I didn't believe he would have left the photos on Jana's windshield for her to find. It seemed too petty for a man who thought so much of himself. I believe he would have gone straight to Tiffany to deliver the news himself, relishing the look on her face when he did it.

And then there was Tiffany's threat, which Landon could have brushed off as nothing more than a lie, a way for her to appear tough and connected when she wasn't.

I had too many questions and not enough answers.

I needed an audience with him right away.

I arrived at the office and walked inside, finding Hunter and Simone hunched over the computer, giggling. Hunter was dressed in a pair of brown corduroy overalls, which matched the color of her braids. Simone was wearing a black blazer over an Erasure T-shirt and dark jeans.

"I could use a good laugh today," I said. "What's so funny?"

"We're watching cat videos," Simone said.

"Montages of cats who knock things off countertops on purpose," Hunter added.

"Sounds like a far more relaxing way to spend the day than what my day has been like," I said. "Shall we talk about the case?"

Simone shot me a wink. "We shall."

We gathered around the sofa, and for the next several minutes, I filled them in on where I'd been and who I'd seen since the last time we spoke.

After I finished, Simone said, "Having met Queenie yesterday, I'm not surprised to hear that she showed up at the coffee shop this morning."

"I feel like she's everywhere."

"I think I know why," Simone said. "Most of the people I talked to in Tiffany's neighborhood think Queenie's taken on an amateur sleuth role, doing a little investigating on her own. She's been to all their houses, taking notes, asking questions. She's even telling people she's going to solve the investigation before anyone else."

"Is she now? She didn't mention that to me. What else did the neighbors have to say?"

"Aside from Queenie, Martha, and Janice, most of them didn't know Tiffany well. They saw her at a few of the neighborhood block parties, which Queenie puts together. Well, she *was* putting them together. Not sure they'll be well attended in the future."

"Has something happened?"

"Many of the neighbors are convinced Queenie hosts the block parties to call them out on things."

"Like what?"

"Having weedy lawns, keeping the trash can out days after trash day, making too much noise after the sun's gone down. They're getting tired of it."

"Tired or not, I bet she gets her way most of the time. She seems relentless. Did you learn anything useful when you met with Tiffany's neighbors?"

Simone pulled out her notebook and flipped a few pages, looking over her notes. "There was only one person who may have heard something around the time of the murder, a little girl. She lives in the house to the right of Tiffany's."

I leaned closer, resting my elbows on my knees. "Tell me about it."

"Her name is Layla. She was playing outside in the back yard, and she's sure she heard a woman scream. As soon as she heard it, she went inside and told her mother, Chelsea."

"What did Chelsea do?"

"You're not going to like the answer. She went to the front yard, and when she didn't hear anyone screaming, she figured Layla was mistaken."

"Chelsea didn't even bother to check and see if Tiffany was okay?"

"She did not. Her baby was sleeping, and she didn't want to leave the kids alone."

"She couldn't be bothered to step away for one minute to go next door and check on her neighbor?"

"I get what you're saying," Simone said. "When I was talking to Chelsea, she seemed a bit frazzled. She has two kids and is pregnant with her third. If the baby wasn't crying, Layla was asking for something. The woman looks like she could use a break."

"Given she lived right next door, did she know Tiffany at all?"

"Not well. They'd just moved into the neighborhood a month ago. She said the first day, Tiffany came over on move-in day and offered to help them unpack, but Chelsea's husband declined the offer. Hours later, when they were still pulling boxes out of the van, Tiffany brought over a pizza, so they wouldn't have to worry about dinner."

It was just like Tiffany, always putting the lives of others over her own.

"Did Tiffany and Chelsea talk since then?" I asked.

"Not much."

"So, Tiffany takes the time to offer her help, and even takes them dinner, but Chelsea couldn't spare one minute to dig a little deeper about a scream she'd heard?"

Simone shrugged. "I understand how you feel. I'm just telling you what she told me."

"I know you are. I just … nowadays people don't check on their neighbors the way they used to do it seems. It's a shame."

"I don't know any of my neighbors," Hunter chimed in. "Couldn't tell you a single one of their names. And that's how I like it."

"If you heard someone scream, you wouldn't investigate?" I asked.

"A scream could mean anything. Could be the neighbor is watching a movie or playing a video game. Or … you know, getting busy."

Maybe I was the odd one out, the person who couldn't hear a sound like that and let it go. I'd need to know, to be certain everything was all right.

I wasn't sure why Chelsea's decision not to check on Tiffany irked me so much. I doubted it would have changed the outcome. If she had gone over to Tiffany's house, there was a big possibility she would have put herself in danger, and maybe even her children.

Switching topics, I turned toward Hunter. "I know I asked you to look into Tiffany's recent clients, but there's only one person I'd like to focus on today—

Landon Fairfax, the soon-to-be ex-husband of Rylie Fairfax, Tiffany's recent client. Have you learned anything about him?"

"I know more about Rylie than I do about Landon. They got married when they were thirty, and now they're in their mid-forties. Landon comes from money. Lots of it. His great-grandfather was a railroad baron. The family's worth billions."

"And Rylie? What's her background?"

"She grew up in a middle-class family. They weren't poor, but they weren't well off, either."

"Where did Landon and Rylie meet?"

"I found an article written a few years ago, talked about how Landon met Rylie at a restaurant when he was in college. She was his waitress."

"I'll bet his parents didn't approve of the match."

"I'm sure you're right. Even if they didn't give their blessing, he still married her."

"Did they have any kids?"

"Nope. When I was searching online, I came across his Instagram profile. From the looks of it, Landon traded her in."

"For a younger model?" Simone asked.

"For an older one. He tagged this new woman in a bunch of photos, so then I started looking into her, because ... well, I just find the entire family so intriguing. The new lady in his life is Vivienne Carrington, and she's in her late fifties."

If Landon's family had enormous wealth, I wondered why he cared so much about coming out on the losing end of the divorce case. Then again, I didn't know the amount they'd settled on.

"Do we know how much Rylie got in the divorce?" I asked.

"What she asked for: three million dollars."

Simone and I exchanged glances.

"From a billionaire?" I asked. "That's it?"

"Yep."

"Three million is a drop in the bucket for his family. Why so little?"

"I don't know. She asked for three million and to have her attorney fees paid."

It didn't make sense.

Why would Landon go to the trouble of threatening Tiffany over what seemed like such a small sum in comparison to his overall worth?

And why did he tell Tiffany his life was ruined?

Hunter lifted a finger. "Oh, I almost forgot. Rylie did ask for one other thing in the settlement. She wanted custody of their dog, Duchess, and she got it."

The dog.

Now there was something.

If Landon had a strong attachment, he may have been infuriated by the court's decision to give custody to Rylie.

As I pondered that thought, my phone rang.

I didn't recognize the number.

"Excuse me a moment," I said.

I answered the call as I walked toward my office. Before I even had the chance to get a word out, a high-pitched voice began shouting into the phone.

"Slow down," I said. "Who is this?"

"Janice."

"What's wrong?"

"It's Queenie. You need to come. You need to come now."

"Why? What's happened?"

I heard what sounded like wailing, followed by, "She's ... she's *dead*."

I stood there in shock, hearing her words but being unable to take them in.

Not three hours ago, I'd seen Queenie. I'd talked to her.

To be told she was dead was almost inconceivable.

"Where are you?" I asked. "And what happened?"

"I … we're …"

The call disconnected, and I hunched over my desk, burying my head in my hands as Simone and Hunter rushed to my side.

"What's going on?" Simone asked.

I looked up, shaking my head as a thought came to mind. "It's Queenie. I'm sorry to say she won't be solving the case before we do."

"Why not?"

"Turns out, she's dead."

25

As I drove to Queenie's house, questions filtered in and out of my mind, my nerves getting the best of me as I thought about the abrupt end to my phone call with Janice. If it turned out Queenie had been murdered, I worried the killer might still be lingering around, putting Janice and Martha's lives in imminent danger.

My fears turned to relief when I turned on Tiffany's street and saw both women standing in front of Queenie's house, consoling each other.

I parked and walked over.

"I apologize about our call getting cut short," Janice said. "A couple of police officers arrived while we were on the phone, and the first thing they did was to escort us out of Queenie's house. They said something about it being necessary for our own safety, but we weren't harming anything by being there. And I would have liked to stay."

Janice failed to see the bigger picture.

"What happened to Queenie?" I asked. "Did someone kill her?"

Janice nodded.

"The reason the police wanted you out of the house was so they could clear it," I said, "and make sure no one else is in there. If the killer was still around when you got here …"

I stopped myself from saying: *You two could have been next.*

Eyes wide, Janice pressed a hand to her chest. "My goodness, we were so caught up in the shock of finding Queenie the way we did, it never occurred to us that someone might still be in the house."

"It's all so … so … unexpected," Martha said, wiping her nose on a handkerchief. "First Tiffany, and now Queenie. And why toss the house and not take anything?"

"Toss the house?"

"Oh, yes. It's an absolute mess."

An ambulance screeched to a stop in front of Queenie's house, and behind it, Whitlock and Foley. Both men acknowledged me with a nod as they exited the vehicle, and then they shifted their focus to Officer Higgins, who was standing in the doorway. Foley and Whitlock made their way to him, speaking with him for a couple of minutes, and then Whitlock came over to me.

He looked at Janice and Martha and tipped his head. "Ladies."

They acknowledged him with nods, and he turned toward me. "Been here long?"

"I arrived just before you."

"What do you know?"

"Same as you, I expect."

Whitlock thumbed at Queenie's house. "Higgins just confirmed the house is clear so we can get going, and I expect Silas will be here any time now."

"Did Higgins say anything else?"

"He confirmed Queenie was murdered."

"Where?"

"In her bedroom."

"How?"

"Another stabbing, though I'm not privy to all the details yet. Thought I'd touch base with you first, let you know we can go in."

I wanted nothing more than to go over and have a look around, but I had questions first—questions only Janice and Martha could answer.

Turning toward them, I said, "I know it's hard and you're both in shock, but I've been wondering about how you came to find Queenie dead in her house."

Martha opened her mouth to speak, whispering, "I don't ... I don't think I can."

Janice draped an arm around Martha, saying, "It's all right. Why don't you let me do the talking?"

Martha sniffled, then nodded.

"Where would you like me to start, Detective?" Janice asked.

"I want to hear about your day today and any interactions you had with Queenie before she died," I said.

"When I woke up this morning, I noticed Queenie's car wasn't in the driveway. Then, around eleven o'clock, she arrived home. I walked over to see where she'd been and what she'd been doing. She was a bit cryptic at first, though she did admit to running into you this morning."

"Did she say anything about our conversation?"

"Not much. She acted surprised to have seen you. We chatted for a few minutes, and she said she was tired and wanted to take a nap. She suggested we get together at her house at one o'clock. We planned to watch a movie."

"What happened next?"

"I arrived at Queenie's house just before one o'clock, and

Martha was already there. She said she'd been knocking for a minute or two, and Queenie hadn't answered. We assumed she might still be asleep, but we weren't sure and decided we'd better check on her."

"How did you get into the house?"

Martha stepped back, her finger drifting toward a garden gnome posed atop a red-and-white polka-dot mushroom. "She keeps a spare key in that silly little thing. We used the key to open the door, but we didn't go in at first."

"Why not?" I asked.

"We thought if we barged in, we might give her a scare. We announced ourselves and waited a moment. When there was no response, we stepped inside and tried again. This time, we heard a sound we believed was coming from the bedroom."

"Tell me about it—what did it sound like?"

"Like someone moaning, which we thought was Queenie at first, but now, knowing what we do, we think it was her cat. We followed the sound to the bedroom, and when I pushed the door open ... I ... I, well, nothing could have prepared me for seeing her in that way—in bed, her shirt stained with blood, knife sticking right out of her chest. We knew there wasn't much hope of her being alive, but still, I checked for a pulse. But there was just *nothing*. No signs of life."

If Janice and Martha saw Queenie at eleven, the timeline for her murder was a tight, two-hour window.

"When you called me, Janice, I was at my office," I said. "Simone, one of the ladies who works for me, said she was here yesterday questioning the neighbors about Tiffany's murder. They said Queenie was investigating Tiffany's murder herself— trying to beat me and the police to solving it."

"I'm sorry to say it's true," Janice said. "We weren't sure whether you knew or not, but once we realized Queenie was dead, we were going to tell you. And we want you to know that we tried to warn her, tried to get her to keep an eye out but not take any action. But as you know, Queenie wasn't the type to take orders from anyone."

It was as I feared, and the cost?

Her life.

"Did Queenie share anything new about the case with you two, anything we should know about?" Whitlock asked.

"She may have been engaged in some sleuthing of her own, but she refused to talk to us about it."

"Why?"

"She didn't care one bit about risking her own safety, but she wasn't about to let her meddling put us in danger too."

"I see, which is why you weren't with her earlier today. She was following one of Tiffany's friends, someone she saw coming out of Tiffany's house this morning. Did she mention him to you?"

"Not to me. Martha?"

Martha shook her head.

"Did Queenie ever mention anyone she considered to be a suspect?" I asked.

"No one. It's like I said before, ever since we talked to you, she kept us in the dark."

I'd gotten more out of Janice than I expected, and looking at both women, I had no desire to carry on with my questioning. After the day they'd had, they needed to relax and grieve together for their dear friend.

"Thank you for talking to us after all you've been through today," I said. "We'll leave you both to get some rest. If you need me for anything, you have my number."

They nodded, and we said our goodbyes.

Once they were out of earshot, Whitlock turned to me. "I wasn't aware Queenie was doing some investigating of her own."

"I wasn't either. I just learned about it. I knew she was fond of being involved in other people's business. But now I believe she was a lot more involved in the case than we realized. I think she stumbled upon something, something that led to her murder."

26

Queenie's home had been ransacked. Drawers and cabinets in the kitchen were open, and everything from paperclips to jewelry was scattered around the floor. I stood silent for a moment, trying to make sense of it all, then stepped into the living room. Foley was hunched over the coffee table, examining what looked like a cocktail ring, which I assumed was Queenie's.

"Seems the murderer may have been looking for something," I said. "I wonder if he found it."

Foley took hold of the ring in his gloved hand and lifted it to the light, and I got a better look at it, and the massive diamond in its center.

"I agree," he said. "If it was a robbery, he'd be an idiot to leave this behind."

"Simone was here yesterday, talking to the neighbors," I said. "She was told Queenie had taken it upon herself to play amateur detective, hoping to solve Tiffany's murder before we did."

He stared at me for a moment, then said, "You got that look

in your eye—the one you always have right before you're about to hit me with a theory. Am I right?"

"You are, I just haven't thought it through all the way yet."

"Go on."

"What if Queenie confronted a few people she considered to be suspects and riled them up, trying to get one of them to confess? With her personality, she could have pushed one too many buttons, leaving the killer feeling like they had no choice but to take her out."

Foley shifted his weight from one foot to the other. "Let's say you're right, even if she threatened people, why would anyone risk a second murder unless she had actual proof of their crime?"

He had a point.

And maybe she did have proof of some sort.

If the motive was to murder her, and nothing more, it didn't seem logical that her house had been turned upside down when Tiffany's hadn't been.

"I just wish Queenie had kept some kind of record of her comings and goings—anything that might tell us what she'd been doing over the past week," I said.

If only ...

Whitlock entered the room, joining us. "I don't know about a record, but I just remembered something. When we first questioned Ron Wheeler about Tiffany, he told us that after he found her in the bathroom, the shock and sorrow of it all was overwhelming. He rushed outside and broke down, vomiting on the lawn. One of Tiffany's neighbors saw the whole thing and came over to see if he was all right. Remember, Foley?"

Foley raised a brow, nodding. "Yeah, now that you mention it. He said it was a woman. He didn't catch her name. We asked him to describe her, and he said she was older, with white hair. After the woman checked on him, she went into Tiffany's house to get him a glass of water. That's when he called the police." He shot me a look. "Had to be Queenie."

It was a crucial piece of information Queenie had neglected to share with me, and it shifted how I saw everything. I now knew she'd been inside Tiffany's house. Had the killer left something behind, an item Queenie discovered?

"I believe the woman who approached Ron that day was Queenie," I said. "If I'm right, she had access to Tiffany's house *before* the police arrived. In that time, she could have taken something, maybe an item she thought didn't belong to Tiffany. If she was talking to our suspects, she may have used it as leverage to get answers."

"You think she was withholding it from us all this time, though?" Foley asked. "We asked every woman on this street if they spoke to Ron that day. They all said no."

One of them was lying, and all signs pointed to Queenie.

"When I first met Queenie, she seemed distraught over Tiffany's death," I said. "But as we started to discuss the investigation, she seemed invigorated, which brings me to my theory."

"I figured we were getting around to it," Foley said. "Let's hear it."

"Think about Queenie's life. She wakes up each day, doing much of the same monotonous routine. Then something scandalous happens—a murder on the street she just happens to live on. A murder that needs to be solved. So Queenie decides to try and outsmart and outwit all of us, getting justice for Tiffany in the process."

"Yes, yes. We know all this, though."

"I'm not finished. It's possible Queenie, while in Tiffany's home, found a clue of some kind. Then she started talking to those she believed capable of the murder. The killer, worried they're about to be caught, decides to shut her up for good.

Then they trash her house looking for … who knows what." I paused, then added, "Well? What do you think? Sounds reasonable to me."

Foley hooked his thumbs into his belt loops. "It's a theory. As for the last part, not sure it's right."

"Not sure it's wrong, either," Whitlock said.

Foley jerked back and, in a teasing tone said, "Taking her side, are we?"

"It's not about sides. It's about how often her theories are correct."

Foley wagged a finger in his direction. "Until it's proven, it's just a theory."

I'd prove it no matter how many hours I had to spend rifling through Queenie's house. If something was here, a clue leading us to the killer, I had to find it.

"I think we should give Ron a call to see if he remembers seeing anything out of place inside the home that day."

"Good idea," Whitlock said. "I'll do it."

"I'd like to pitch in and help you gather evidence, see what we can find around here," I said. "I'm here. May as well let me join in."

"Given the condition of this place, we could use all the help we can get," Whitlock said. "And you, of all people, knows she has an exceptional eye for finding clues."

Foley looked at me, then at Whitlock, then around Queenie's place. "Oh, I suppose it's all right. If you find anything good, bring it straight to me. Am I clear?"

"Clear as a foggy mirror," I said, smacking him on the shoulder. "I'm kidding, of course. And hey, thanks for letting me stay."

"Hard to know where to start in all this mess," Foley said.

"Before I get started, Silas arrived several minutes ago, and I'd like to speak to him."

"Sure, he's in the back bedroom. Talk to him, and then we'll see what *theories* you come up with next."

He laughed when he said it, though I detected a hint of sarcasm.

We parted ways, and I headed toward Queenie's room, finding Silas crouched over her body when I entered. Her room was in shambles, much like the rest of the house.

Queenie was lying on the bed, face up, dressed in a pastel blouse and a pair of loose cargo pants. Her hands were at her sides. There was a fair amount of blood, but it didn't come close to what I'd witnessed in Tiffany's bathroom.

"What's this theory I'm hearing you all talking about out there?" Silas asked.

"Queenie was inside Tiffany's house after she was murdered, *before* the police arrived. At first, it seemed strange to me that Tiffany's house wasn't tossed like Queenie's. But Queenie was running her own investigation into Tiffany's murder. Put two and two together and ..."

"She put a target on her back."

"A big one. I think her killer was here, looking for something."

"Could be."

I shifted my gaze to the stab wound on Queenie's chest. "Have you noticed any similarities between the two murders, anything to suggest we're looking at the same killer?"

"Some similar, some not so similar." He pointed out the chest wound, adding, "Based on the angle in which Tiffany was stabbed, it suggests the killer is right-handed. I see a similar angle in the way Queenie was stabbed. But there's one big difference."

"What is it?"

"Queenie got a knife straight to the heart—one and done. Tiffany was stabbed multiple times."

I considered what might have set the two murders apart. "Tiffany's murder may have been a crime of passion, someone working out anger and rage, whereas Queenie's could have been carried out of sheer necessity. What can you tell me about the knife sticking out of her chest?"

"It matches a set Higgins found in one of the kitchen drawers."

"Just like last time, the killer arrived on the scene, used what was available, and then left the murder weapon."

"Seems careless to me."

Or the work of a person who didn't believe they'd ever get caught.

"You scraped Tiffany's fingernails," I said. "Find anything?"

"Not a thing. Oh, and I can confirm, she wasn't sexually assaulted."

It was a relief.

To be murdered was bad enough. To be assaulted at the same time ... I couldn't imagine it.

"Is there anything else you can tell me?" I asked.

"Kiera's working on lifting some prints off those photos you were given. Should know something anytime. You gonna be here a while?"

"Foley's allowed me to help them gather evidence," I said. "I'll circle back in a while to see if you've made any other discoveries."

"Alrighty."

He gave me a two-finger salute, and I left the room.

Before I began to collect any potential evidence, I decided to do a full walkthrough of the house, hoping I'd see something that piqued my interest.

I started in the kitchen, peering inside the open drawers and cabinets. It was easy to see which ones had been messed around with and which ones hadn't. The untouched cabinets and drawers were in perfect order, not a single item out of place. The rest were a scattered mess, with items being tossed out, strewn all over the floor. On the far end of the kitchen, the back door stood slightly ajar.

The killer's escape, perhaps?

I walked to the living room next, but there wasn't much to see. A small television rested atop a table that looked like it may have doubled at one time as a TV tray. There was a sofa and a couple of chairs, all covered with plastic. On the wall behind the sofa was a painting of Queenie standing beside a man. I wondered if he was her late husband.

Moving to the back of the house, I entered the guest room. Aside from the bed, there was a nightstand and two dressers. I looked around the drawers, all of which were shut. Peered into the closet too. What struck me as odd was that everything seemed untouched.

Had the killer been interrupted during his search?

I thought about the tight timeline between the conversation Queenie had with her friends when she arrived home, and Janice and Martha's arrival at one o'clock.

The killer may have been forced to make a quick escape, fleeing out the back door.

Having found nothing of note thus far, I located Foley and asked how I could be of the most help. They'd started placing number cards around anything they considered to be relevant. I was assigned to take photos of those items, so they could be bagged and tagged and taken into evidence.

A few hours later, we hadn't made any brilliant discoveries, putting a damper on my theory. Whitlock tried calling Ron, but Ron didn't answer. He'd left a message asking him to call back.

Overall, I was feeling a bit deflated.

All the pieces had started to fit together so perfectly in my mind.

I'd felt sure I was right, that we were getting somewhere.

But now ... I wasn't as sure.

Maybe I was grasping at anything because I hadn't yet had a break in the case. It happened, I knew—though not usually to me.

I was tired, and of all the poor choices I'd made that day, the worst had been my decision to wear high-heeled shoes. They were adorable, of course, a shiny, black, round-toed pair from the '20s, which complimented my black-and-cream flapper-style day dress. But after standing almost all day, I was tempted to go barefoot.

I wiggled my toes and sighed. My thoughts turned to heading home. I longed for a nice, hot shower, followed by the comfort of my bed, alongside Giovanni and Luka. Deciding it was time to call it a day, I went looking for Foley. I'd taken a single step inside the guest room when one of my heels caught on a piece of carpet, and I tripped, falling face first to the ground. For a moment, I just lay there, catching my breath.

The fall had caused a clatter, no doubt echoing throughout the house, and within seconds, Foley and Whitlock rushed into the room.

"Are you all right?" Whitlock asked.

"A little embarrassed, but I'm fine, yes," I said. "I chose the wrong shoes to wear today."

"I've always wondered how you do it, investigating in some of the outfits you wear," Foley said. "Can't be easy."

He reached for my hand, and as I went to take it, I hesitated, my eyes coming to rest on a piece of carpet in the corner of the room. It looked different than the rest, uneven and loose. It was almost as if it hadn't been laid right in that area, or it had, and it loosened up over time.

"I just got off the phone with Ron, and you're right, Georgiana, he did see something unusual on the day of the murder," Whitlock said.

"Hold that thought," I said. "I need to check something first."

I scooted to the other side of the room and reached for the piece of carpet. Tugging at the corner, it started to pull right up. I then tugged at another piece a few feet away. It wouldn't budge. I brought myself to my knees, eyeing the rest of the carpet in the room. No other areas stood out, which I found curious.

"Mind sharing what you're doing with us?" Foley asked.

"This patch of carpet is loose."

"It's an older house. The carpet is old too. I bet it hasn't been replaced in decades from the looks of it."

I turned, reaching for the loose patch and lifting it higher so I could see beneath. Bending over, I slapped a hand to my lips, shocked at what I saw.

"What is it?" Whitlock asked.

A stroke of luck had led me to Queenie's super-secret hiding place.

I lifted the carpet again. Before me was a notecard, my name written in cursive on the front.

Next to the card was something unique.

I glanced over at Whitlock. "Just now, you said Ron saw something unusual at Tiffany's. Was it a lighter?"

Whitlock blinked in surprise. "Yeah, how'd you know?"

27

I waved Foley and Whitlock over, tipping my head toward the discovery I made.

"Well, I'll be," Foley said. "I can't believe it."

"And the card, with your name on it," Whitlock said. "Eerie. It's like she knew you'd find it."

I reached for the card, unfolded it, and read aloud.

To the person reading this note,

If you are not Mrs. Georgiana Germaine of the Case Closed Detective Agency this note is NOT for you. I would ask that you cease reading immediately and see that she gets the note and the accompanying lighter at your earliest convenience.

Now then ...

Georgiana,

If you are reading this, it means I am dead. What a pity, though I've lived a long life, a good life, a life with almost no regret. If you were the one to discover my hiding place, you're a far better detective than I gave you credit for, my dear, and I'm sorry for ever doubting you.

I also must apologize for not handing over the lighter sooner. As I'm sure you're aware, Tiffany was not a smoker, so it seemed unlikely that the lighter belonged to her. I imagine the killer dropped it at some point. Please note what appears to be dried blood on its side.

When I entered Tiffany's house on the day she was murdered, I found the lighter on top of the rug in the kitchen. My glasses weren't on when I picked it up, so I didn't notice the blood at first. The lighter itself is vintage and unique. I did some research, and it turns out, a similar one by the same maker sold at auction for over a thousand dollars earlier this year.

After I found the lighter, I slipped it into a plastic bag, and I considered looking around the rest of the house. Before I had the chance, Tiffany's father found me in the kitchen. He told me the police were on their way, and I fisted my hand around the lighter. That's when an idea came to mind. How challenging would it be to see if I could solve the murder myself?

A challenge I decided to accept.

I bet you're wondering why I'd do such a thing, but there's something you don't know about me. Before I was married, I was a police officer, the first female officer in my city. I had dreams of becoming a detective one day. Back then, women weren't promoted to those roles, even though I would have run circles around them.

As on officer, I didn't get to play much with the big boys, either. I was given menial tasks like supervising women and children in custody and investigating domestic abuse. A couple of years into the job, I met my husband. He was shocked to hear I had a job, and even more so when I explained my position. He didn't want a wife who worked. He wanted a wife who stayed at home with the kids, a wife who had dinner waiting when he came through the door. If I was to marry him, I had to choose—him or the job. I quit my job, but the desire to do detective work never left me. And though we tried, children were never in the cards for us.

In closing, I bet you're wondering if I was able to identify the killer before my death. I'll say this much; I have a solid idea, but after meeting you and knowing the personal connection you have to this case, I have a feeling you'd rather solve it yourself. So, I'll not speak any further on the matter. After all, if I gave away the name of my prime suspect, what mystery would be left to solve?

Farewell, Detective, and best of luck to you,

Queenie

I slid the letter into my pocket, and for a moment, the three of us stood there in shock, as if searching for the right words to say.

"What a cunning, if not clever, woman," Whitlock said.

"Cunning, yes," Foley said. "Clever? She got herself killed—and for what—a one-time opportunity to relive a career she wished she hadn't given up?"

"I disagree," I said. "I believe she exited this life achieving a dream she never thought possible."

Foley stepped in front of me and bent down, lifting the plastic bag out of Queenie's hiding place and dangled it in front of us. We all leaned in, taking a closer look. The front of the lighter was fashioned in black lacquer with a chrome finish on the front, and on the back, cedarwood. And just as Queenie said, there was a spot of what appeared to be dried blood.

"Thoughts?" Foley asked.

"It's feminine enough to belong to a woman and yet masculine enough to be owned by a man," I said.

"I agree," Whitlock said.

Foley turned toward Whitlock. "Would you holler at Silas, see if we can borrow him for a moment?"

"You got it."

Whitlock left the room, and I pulled my cell phone out of my pocket. "Before you take the lighter into evidence, I'd like to take a few photos of it."

"Go right ahead."

I took my photos, then Whitlock and Silas entered the room.

Silas looked at the bag and said, "Whatcha got there?"

"A lighter, and a crazy note that accompanied it," Foley said. "Georgiana, why don't you do the honors?"

I showed Silas the letter, who read through it with a look of astonishment. Then I explained how I came to find both items.

When I finished, he leaned over, peering into the plastic bag. "I find the smudge mark confusing."

"How so?"

"Let's assume it's blood, either Tiffany's or the killers. How do we think it got there?"

It was a question I'd thought of myself, and I had a few ideas.

"I assume the killer would have gotten a fair amount of Tiffany's blood on himself during her murder," I said. "Maybe he went to the kitchen to wash off before he left," I said. "There were what appeared to be dried red spots on the rug in front of the sink."

"If he wore gloves, why bother going to the sink?"

"True, but Tiffany's blood could have gotten beneath the gloves, or all over his person."

"I see where you're going ... in the process of cleaning up, the lighter may have slipped out of his pocket," Foley said. "It could have made contact with blood on his skin or on his clothing as it fell to the ground."

"I'd bet the killer didn't even realize he'd dropped the lighter," I said. "It's small and lightweight. When he figured it out, it was too late. Police were crawling all over the place."

Silas nodded, and his cell phone rang to the tune of Aerosmith's "Walk This Way."

He reached into his pocket and left the room.

"If Queenie started talking to people she thought were connected to the murder, there are only so many people she would have known about," Foley said.

"I … ahh, regret to admit, but I may have spilled a bit too much tea when I spoke to her," Whitlock said. "She had a way of getting information out of a person. I believe I said too much."

"Let that be a lesson to you," Foley warned.

Whitlock nodded and yawned, and Foley followed suit.

"I'm ready to call it a day," I said.

"I'm right there with you," Foley said. "Let's go home, get some shut-eye, and touch base with each other tomorrow."

Good idea.

It was almost midnight, and every fiber of my being had started to ache.

We made our way over to our vehicles, and as they backed away, I leaned against my car, taking a moment to assess the day. Turning toward Tiffany's house, it was still hard to accept my friend was gone. There would be no more dinners here, no celebrations, no laughs. The longer I stood there, thinking about it, the bigger the lump in my throat became.

It was one of those moments where life offered up an icy, unwanted little nudge, a nudge that reminded me just how short life could be and how important it was to stay in contact with those who held space in our innermost circles.

The front door opened, and Silas burst out, his face frantic.

He looked left, then right, then his eyes met mine.

"Have Foley and Whitlock gone?" he asked.

"A few minutes ago. What's wrong?"

"I have news. I just got a call from Kiera. She managed to lift a few decent prints from the pictures you gave us."

The ones left on Jana Seymour's car. "Fantastic. What do you know?"

"The first two prints were a match to Jana."

"And the third?"

"Belongs to a guy named Chad Hayes. Name mean anything to you?"

Chad Hayes.

Well, well … it sure did.

"I know him," I said. "He dated Tiffany a while back and then a second time, right before she met Tyler."

"Oh, man. We gotta let Foley and Whitlock know."

We did.

But …

"Would you mind if I told them?" I asked.

"Not at all. It would check one more thing off my list."

I was glad Silas hadn't asked *when* I planned on telling them.

I would tell them.

I just needed to make a stop first.

28

I'd been banging on the door of Chad's apartment for what seemed like several minutes, though in reality, it hadn't been that long.

"Open the door, Chad," I said. "Your car's in the driveway, and your lights are on. I know you're here."

The door opened moments later, and I was taken aback to see it *wasn't* Chad. A woman stood before me, her long hair a tangled mess. Her face was flushed, like she'd been running and was out of breath. A navy-colored sheet was draped around what appeared to be her naked body, making it clear my arrival had come as somewhat of an interruption.

She blew a lock of hair off her face and glared at me. "Do you have any idea what time it is right now?"

"I'm aware. I need to speak with Chad. Where is he?"

"He's in the bathroom, lady. Look, I don't know what you're doing here in the middle of the night, but he's busy. To make myself clear, he's not accepting visitors right now."

She'd made herself clear.

Now it was my turn to return the favor.

I leaned around her, shouting, "Chad, get out here. *Now.*"

Unhappy, the woman spread her arms, and the sheet fluttered to the ground. For a moment, she looked embarrassed, and I thought she'd pick it up.

She didn't, though.

She stood her ground, and part of me respected her for it, but if she thought she was going to prevent me from entering Chad's apartment, she was about to learn a new life lesson.

"I'll give you one chance to get out of my way," I said. "You should take it."

"Oh, yeah? Or what? Like I said … you're not coming in."

I grabbed her arm, wrenching it behind her back as she yelped in pain, and I wasn't even pulling, not hard. I pushed her to the side and entered the apartment, releasing her arm as I said, "Don't even think about coming at me."

But she'd already thought about it, and she rushed toward me, fists raised. As she attempted to land a punch, I jerked back, and she stepped forward, tripping over my heeled shoe and falling over the back of the couch.

"I warned you," I said. "Do yourself a favor and stay down."

I didn't think she'd heed that advice, but before she had the chance to make another bad decision, Chad rushed downstairs.

"What in the … Georgiana? What are you doing here? And Lacey, why is your naked body bent over my couch?"

Lacey brought herself to a sitting position, grabbing a couple of couch pillows and placing them in front of her to cover up. She shot me dagger eyes, saying, "It's *her* fault. *She's* the crazy one, not me. Who is she, one of your ex-girlfriends?"

"Uh, no," I said. "Not even close."

I walked back to where the sheet had fallen and picked it up, tossing it at her.

"Gee, thanks," she said.

Then I glanced at Chad. "We need to talk."

"We need to talk, all right. Showing up at a person's house

in the middle of the night just because you're working an investigation is not cool, not cool at all."

"What are you talking about?" Lacey asked. "What investigation?"

Chad squeezed his eyes shut, sighing. "Remember me telling you about my ex-girlfriend, the one who was just murdered? Georgiana is one of the investigators."

Lacey raised a brow, her expression softening. "*You're* the friend."

"I'm the friend," I said.

"Well, hey … ahh, sorry about Tiffany, but Chad's right. You shouldn't barge in at this hour."

"It's not something I do often. This couldn't wait."

"*What* couldn't wait?" Chad asked.

"We should talk in private."

"Whatever it is, I don't see why Lacey can't hear it. I have nothing to hide."

Understatement of the year, right there.

"Don't you?" I asked.

"What's that supposed to mean?"

"You want to talk in front of her? Fine," I said. "Before Tiffany died, you were following her. You took pictures. Then you left those pictures on Tyler's wife's car."

He cocked his head back, laughing. "No, I didn't."

"Yes, you did. And if you're lying to me about that, what else are you lying about?"

"I don't know what you think you know—"

"I don't *think* I know anything. Fingerprints can be lifted off paper. It isn't easy, but it's possible. When I met Tyler's wife, Jana, she gave me the photos you took, the ones you left on the car. I handed them over to the lab for testing. About thirty minutes ago, I learned three prints were lifted. Two belonged to Jana, and the third, to you."

"How would my prints even be identified? I've never ..." He slapped a hand to his forehead. "I ... ahh, I just remembered. I got pulled over once when I was thirteen for driving my dad's car to La Salita Loca. So dumb. The cop was being a jerk, and I threw a taco at him."

"You threw a taco at a police officer?"

"Yeah, and I was arrested for it. It was so stressful, and it happened so long ago, I forgot all about being fingerprinted."

"Thanks for the story, but you still lied to me. I want to know why."

Chad glanced at Lacey, thumbing at the door. "Sorry, babe. Georgiana's right. We should speak in private. I'll see you tomorrow, all right?"

Lacey shot up from the couch. "Are you kidding me?" Furious, she rushed upstairs, spewing curse words as she hurled items down the stairs—a brush, a pillow, a hoodie, a bag of chips.

As she continued to curse and bang things around upstars, I looked around, impressed with the overall look of his home. It was a lot nicer than I'd expected, and the furniture looked high-end. It was also one of the cleanest homes I'd ever been in, not a speck of dust anywhere.

Lacey came back down and snatched a duffel bag sitting on a chair. Shoving her belongings inside it, she slung the bag over her shoulder, offering Chad a dirty look as she sped to the door. "This is the last time, Chad! The *last* time. You hear me?"

The door slammed shut behind her, and he swished a hand through the air. "She says it's the last time, every time. It's not. But man, I should have bummed a smoke from her before she left. I could use one."

"Who is she, anyway?"

"One of my coworkers. We've known each other for years. It's not serious. More like friends with benefits, you know?"

I didn't know.

I'd never had one of those.

"You sure she's not more into you than you are into her?" I asked.

"We tried to be more than friends once. It wasn't good."

I moved a hand to my hip. "Let's talk about the photos and the fact you lied to me. What have you got to say for yourself?"

"I'm sorry?"

"Sorry is a good start. Why lie in the first place?"

"I don't know. I thought about telling you when I first saw you, and then I got all in my head about how you'd feel if I did—like I'm a suspect. You believe me when I say I'm innocent, don't you?"

"How can I?"

"I could never do something so awful. Not just to Tiffany, to anyone."

In truth, even though he'd lied to me, I wanted to believe him.

I was also sure he still loved Tiffany, and not in the *if I can't have you, no one will* kind of way.

But was I wrong?

"Back to the photos," I said. "I have an idea of what you were hoping to achieve. Still, I'd like to hear it."

He nodded and dropped down on the couch. "After Tiffany broke up with me, I couldn't stop thinking about her, and *him*, the guy who swooped in and made a train wreck of the life we were trying to rebuild. So yeah, I followed them a few times, and I took some photos."

"Wasn't it painful, to watch the woman you love with another man?"

"More than you know."

"But you did it anyway."

"There was something about the guy, something *off*. I

thought it was just my jealousy of him at first. But the feeling never went away. It lingered until the night I decided to follow him home. A woman greeted him at the door, and they kissed."

"And you realized he was being unfaithful."

He crossed his arms. "Yeah, but I didn't know if he was seeing two women at the same time, or if one was his wife, the other a mistress, or what. I did an internet search of the address, and it came right up, Tyler and Jana Seymour, and I knew he was married."

"Why not go to Tiffany, tell her what you found out?"

"I would have had to admit I'd been following her around, spying on her."

"So, you decided to let Tyler's wife be the bad guy."

"I thought it was a better plan. Tyler's wife deserved to know, just like Tiffany did. I put the photos on Jana's car, figuring it would do the trick, and I was right. That night when Tyler showed up at Tiffany's, they fought. He cried. She cried. And he left, angry. I hoped it was over."

I had to admit, it was the smarter play.

Jana did what he hoped she'd do—confronted Tiffany about Tyler.

And the best part?

Neither Jana nor Tiffany knew who left the photos, leaving Chad in the clear.

"I'm surprised you didn't swoop in, saving the day," I said.

He shrugged. "I thought it was better to give her time to process it all. Thinking back on that decision now, I realize time was the one thing we didn't have."

"You couldn't have predicted what happened."

He sighed. "Well, there you have it. The whole story."

"You were seen one night, taking photos. Except you were in a black truck, but you drive a car."

"The truck is my dad's. I thought if I was in my car, she'd

recognize me. And hey, if you see Jana again, tell her I'm sorry. I'm sure those photos caused her pain. I was just trying to help her see the truth about her husband."

She saw it.

And for whatever reason, she wanted him back.

"I just have one more question before I go," I said.

"Shoot."

"Has a woman named Queenie come to see you?"

"I was just about to mention her. Yes, she did. She got right in my face, drilling me with questions about Tiffany, asking me where I was at the time of the murder. She told me the police were busy with the case and asked her to come out of retirement to assist. Is that true?"

"It isn't. Queenie was Tiffany's neighbor. She'd started conducting her own investigation into the murder."

"What do you mean she *was* Tiffany's neighbor?"

"She's dead. She was murdered in her home earlier today."

"Two murders on the same street in one week? That's crazy."

"Did she show you anything when she came to see you?"

"Yeah, a photo of a lighter on her cell phone. She said it was found at the crime scene and that it has a bloody fingerprint on it."

A lighter was found, yes.

But it was a smear, not a fingerprint.

"What else did she say?" I asked.

"She claimed the lighter was mine and said the police were closing in. If I admitted to Tiffany's murder, I might be able to strike a deal in exchange for my confession."

It explained why she was dead.

She'd tried to coerce a confession.

Had Chad been the only one she'd accused?

If there were others, had she used the same tactic on everyone?

Those answers would have to wait until tomorrow.

If I was going to be on top of my game, I needed sleep.

"I'm going to head out," I said.

"Hang on a minute."

"What is it?"

"The lighter isn't mine, and everything I just told you is true. I hope it makes up for, you know … not telling you the truth before."

"I have a lot to think about. The police will want to speak with you the first chance they get. When you do, don't lie to them."

29

I slept in until nine, waking to find a note on my nightstand from Giovanni. He'd taken Luka to the park and had made me a souffle, which was waiting for me in the oven. I grabbed my robe out of the closet and walked to the kitchen, pleased to find the souffle was still warm. As I ate at the bar, I made my game plan for the day. Goal one was to meet with Landon Fairfax, the man who'd accused Tiffany of ruining his life.

After learning about him a day before, I'd asked Hunter to get some information on him. I was now the proud recipient of his phone number, address, and a few other pertinent details. Hunter had also been in touch with Tiffany's former client, Rylie Fairfax, who filled her in on Landon's daily routine.

I drove to a popular cycling trail that he biked around almost every morning, hoping I wasn't too late. I parked, waited a while, and then I spotted two men, one fitting the description Hunter had given me. He was lifting a bike over a rack onto the back of a high-end truck. Mission accomplished, he turned to the man next to him and gave him a high-five. The men parted ways, and I exited the car, hurrying over to catch him before he left.

He looked, in a word, douchey, as expected—clad in a sleek, bright, form-fitting jersey that hugged his torso. His padded cycling shorts were tight, ending mid-thigh, and they did the perfect job of emphasizing his muscular quads.

I approached, saying, "Landon Fairfax?"

He seemed startled as he looked my way, but as our eyes met, a flirtatious smile formed. "Who's asking?"

"My name is Georgiana Germaine, and I—"

"I know who you are."

"You do?"

"I've been following the case, or should I say, my people have been following it for me."

His people.

A way of establishing his status from the get-go.

We were off to a smug-worthy start.

"And what have your *people* reported so far?" I asked.

"Let's just say I know just about all there is to know about the case. From what I hear, you're a tenacious one. I'm glad to meet you."

He extended a hand.

I looked at it, but I wasn't in the mood to shake.

"Before Tiffany died, you threatened her," I said.

"I'm aware."

"You said she ruined your life."

He leaned against the truck. "I may have been a bit more dramatic than I intended, but in a way, she did ruin it. What's your point?"

"Your threat places you at the center of my investigation."

"I suppose it does."

We stared at each other, blinking in turn, neither of us saying a word.

"I expected you to be a lot more defensive," I said.

"Why should I be? I knew I'd be questioned, by you and the police, which is the exact reason I have people keeping tabs on what's going on."

"What do you mean by 'keeping tabs'?"

"I'd prefer not to answer."

I moved my hands to my hips. "And I'd prefer you did."

He let out a low, chilling laugh. "It's in my best interest to know what rabbit holes you and the police, are going down. I see the dangling carrot has led to me at last. Six days. I'll admit, I thought I'd see you sooner. If you've concluded I was in some way involved in Tiffany's murder, I regret to inform you the carrot has fallen from your stick. You're raising it at the wrong man."

I was beginning to tire of his carrot-and-stick analogy.

"Why did you confront Tiffany in the way you did?" I asked.

He slid a hand inside his pocket, removed some lip balm, and applied it to his lips. "After Tiffany won in court, my relationship with Vivienne, the woman I was dating, fell apart."

It surprised me.

"Why? With the case in the rear view, the divorce could finalize, and you and Vivienne could move forward."

"You'd think so, but she ended the relationship."

"And you ... what? Blamed Tiffany? It makes no sense. Rylie didn't ask for much in the divorce—a few million. A drop in the bucket compared to your family's overall worth."

He shook his head. "You think I was upset over the money?"

"Weren't you?"

"I would have given her the money she wanted and more, if she'd asked for it."

"Then what was the problem?"

"It was the way she tried to slander my reputation in court, going on and on about the husband I once was, the man she thought she'd be with forever. She topped it off by discussing my 'numerous' affairs."

"Did you have numerous affairs?"

"I slipped up on occasion. Who doesn't?"

"I don't."

"Then you wouldn't understand. It's not like I woke up one day and decided to have an affair when everything in my marriage was fine. Affairs, they have a way of creeping up on you. One day you're making a polite comment to a woman. The next, you're flirting. Before you know it, you wake up one morning, and they're in your bed, or you're in theirs. Infidelity's been around since the dawn of time, and it always will be."

I wasn't sure how to take his candor.

It disgusted and astonished me at the same time, for all the wrong reasons.

"Rylie was stating the obvious and speaking her truth. Why did it bother you so much?" I asked. "Were you worried about your reputation? You don't seem like the kind of person who cares what anyone else thinks."

He bit down on his bottom lip. "I do when it comes to Vivienne. She was in court the day the affairs were mentioned. I didn't even know she planned to be there. She was sitting at the back, taking it all in. Afterward, when I had a chance to talk to her, she was furious. I hadn't told her about the affairs. I tried to explain. I told her Rylie was lying."

"But she wasn't lying. You admitted as much to me just now."

"To you, I admitted it, because it's true. When it comes to the women I'm in relationships with, you say what you need to say to protect yourself and the relationship. Right?"

Wrong.

"I have no reason to lie to you, and I haven't," he continued. "None of it matters now, though. I thought Vivienne was the one woman who could keep me loyal. But I've met someone else, someone even better."

"Why would you take your anger out on Tiffany over your wife's words in court?"

"Because they weren't *her* words. Rylie's an introvert, a woman who doesn't like to stir up drama. I expected her to fight for what she wanted—the money, the dog—and leave everything else out of it. We'd discussed it prior. She wasn't going to mention the affairs. Then Tiffany got to her, and she grew a backbone."

I clenched my fists at my sides, the urge to strike him so overwhelming I had to dig my nails into my palms to stop myself.

"How unfortunate it is when a woman grows a backbone," I said. "I can see now why it angered you to the point of verbal harassment and threats. You have a massive narcissistic ego."

"I didn't harass her."

"Who's the liar now?"

"I was furious that day, I'll admit. Thinking back, I don't even remember what I said. It happens sometimes when I'm angry. I lash out without thinking. If it came across as harassment, she twisted my words because that's not what happened."

I could feel my heart thump, thump, thumping inside my chest.

Faster and faster.

If I was to retain my composure, the topic of conversation needed to shift before I lost the ability to control myself.

"Have you been visited by an elderly woman about the murder investigation?" I asked.

"Ah, yes. Queenie, I believe. She claimed to be assisting the police with the investigation, which we both know is far from the truth."

"Did she tell you about the lighter that was found at Tiffany's house on the day of the murder?"

"She mentioned it."

"Did she accuse you of murdering Tiffany?"

"She did."

"What did you say?"

"I found the whole thing comical. The woman was senile. I bet she had no idea what she was getting herself into. If she had, maybe she wouldn't be dead."

"I didn't find her to be senile, though I'll admit she was out of her depth."

He blew out a long sigh. "I'm not saying she asked for it, but she brought it on, and someone saw to it that she was shut down. Now then, I've enjoyed this little conversation of ours, but it's time for me to go. If there's nothing more ..."

Bite your tongue, Georgiana.

He's not worth it.

"If you've done your research on me, you know my track record," I said.

"I have, and it's impressive, for a—"

"*Woman?*"

He pointed a finger gun at me, then clicked his thumb like he'd pulled the trigger. "Your words, not mine."

"I'm closing in on Tiffany's killer. I can feel it. If it turns out its you, it won't matter how many spies you have running around town. I'll be coming for you, and not even you will be able to stop me."

Pleased with my parting remark, I spun around, signaling an end to our conversation. I hadn't taken a single step forward when I felt it—a quick, stinging smack across my backside.

I whipped around.

The time for keeping my composure was over.

Grinning, he said, "I have no doubt you'll solve the case. That's the spirit!"

My hand sliced through the air and landed on his cheek with a *crack!*—red fingerprints blooming in its wake.

I hadn't felt that satisfied with myself in some time.

"If you ever lay a hand on me again, you'll lose it," I spat.

"I was just teasing. Lighten up."

Leaning forward, I drilled a finger into his chest. "It's no wonder you can't keep a woman. You don't know how to treat one."

"Careful, now. I could report this little harassment of yours to the police."

"You won't."

"And why's that?"

"You may think you know about me, sure—and about my interest in the investigation—but that little stunt with my rearend tells me you missed researching one crucial detail: my husband. You should ask your people to do a little digging on him while they're at it. My husband's family ... well, they're a fascinating read. One might even say frightening. Not for me, but certainly for a scumbag like you."

30

The way I saw it, there were four major suspects in Tiffany's murder. The first, and most obvious was Tyler, whose motive centered around the woman he'd lost and couldn't live without. When Tiffany dismissed him and all possibility of a future together, had his sorrow turned to rage?

Then there was Tyler's wife, Jana. If she were the killer, the clever move would have been for her to eliminate Tiffany without ever revealing she knew about the affair, thus seeming innocent. Instead, she'd gone to Tiffany, discussing her knowledge of the affair in public. Killing her at that point wouldn't have been a smart move.

And while many lies had been told, the biggest of them all was still Tyler's affair.

Moving on to suspect three, Chad seemed like the least likely of the candidates. But the more I considered how sloppy the murders were—impulsive, in broad daylight, lacking a great deal of planning—the more my thoughts kept drifting back to him. He, too, could have had a similar motive to Tyler. Twice they'd tried dating, and twice he'd been rejected. Had the sting of being cast aside for another man been more than he could bear?

My fourth suspect was the arrogant Landon Fairfax, a man I'd come to loathe after a mere ten minutes together. I wanted nothing more than for him to be the murderer.

But was he?

I got the impression losing his temper was a regular part of his routine, something he did more often than not.

I considered those possibilities and more as my cell phone rang. I put the call on speaker, and Whitlock said, "Georgiana, you there?"

He sounded out of breath and tense, unlike his usual jovial self.

"I'm here," I said.

"Where are you right now?"

"I've just left San Simeon, and I'm heading back to Cambria. I just got finished talking to Landon Fairfax, and—"

"Hate to interrupt, but you're going to want to get over to Jana Seymour's house as soon as you can."

"Why? What's happened? Is she all right?"

"Jana's fine. It's Tyler. He's dead."

31

I arrived at Jana's house to find Tyler face down on the living room floor. He'd been shot once in the head. Jana was a few feet away, lying flat atop a stretcher. It appeared she had been shot as well. A tourniquet had been wrapped around her left leg. As I approached, a female paramedic draped a blanket over Jana, then gave Foley a quick nod. Foley nodded back, and, with a slight curl of his finger, motioned for me to come over.

I did, and we entered the hallway.

"What happened?" I asked.

"Hold on a second." He turned toward the paramedic. "Look, I know you need to get her to the hospital, but I want you to hold off for a minute."

"We should get going," she said. "How long do you need?"

Based on Foley's expression, he didn't appreciate her response.

"To clarify, it wasn't a request," he said. "You said it yourself: Jana's fine. Whether you leave right this second or three minutes from now, it won't make a dang bit of difference. Go attend to her. I'll be with you in a minute."

She frowned and turned, and Foley's attention moved back to me.

"I haven't been here long," he said. "I'm not certain about what happened yet."

"What do you know?"

"Forty-five minutes ago, we received a frantic call from Jana. She said Tyler had been shot. She didn't know whether he was alive or dead. When we arrived, he was dead."

"Where was she?"

"On the floor beside him, sobbing over his body."

"Has she said anything to you?"

"Not a word. Every time I ask her a question; all I get is waterworks."

I assumed he was telling me these things for a reason.

"Is there anything I can do to help?" I asked.

"I need to be here, but I'd like you to go with her to the hospital. Once the doctor checks her out, see if you can get her to talk. I want to know everything that happened here."

Foley told the paramedic I'd be coming along for the ride, and I hopped in the back of the van. On the way to the hospital, Jana stayed silent, staring straight ahead as tears continued to stream down her face.

When we arrived at the hospital, the doctor inspected and cleaned the entry and exit wounds, ordered x-rays, and started Jana on antibiotics.

Then it was my turn.

I entered the room, and she put her phone down.

"I didn't mean to interrupt," I said.

"You're fine. I was just talking to my mom."

"I'm sure your family is worried."

"Yeah, my mother lives in Colorado. She's trying to find a flight. I told her she didn't have to come. I'm sure she will anyway."

She turned, staring out the window. "I think I ... I might be in trouble."

"Why?" I asked.

She looked at me, but the words didn't come.

If I was going to get her to talk, I needed to put her at ease.

I took a seat on a chair next to her.

"I feel like I can't breathe," she said.

"You're in shock. It's understandable. In times like this, when I get stressed, there's a little breathing exercise I do. We could do it together if you'd like."

She reached over, grabbing a tissue from the box on the side table and blotting her eye. "I can try. What do you want me to do?"

"We're going to take a deep breath in, hold the breath for a few seconds, and then breathe it out."

She nodded, and I squeezed her hand, hoping the solidarity I was showing would work in my favor.

After a few cleansing breaths, she said, "My mouth feels like it's full of cotton. Would you mind getting me some water?"

I reached for a plastic water jug with the hospital's logo on the front and walked to the sink. I filled it to the top and handed it to her. "I'm not sure if you're up for it, but if you are, can you tell me what happened this morning?"

She took a few sips of water and then pressed a tissue to her nose.

"Tyler showed up at the house this morning," she said. "When I met him at the door, he said he wanted to talk. He seemed fine, in a decent mood. I thought maybe he was doing better and had come over to talk about ending our separation."

"You thought he was going to suggest moving back in together?"

"I did, and I was wrong. So wrong. As soon as I let him

inside and the door closed, he got right in my face, shouting and hurling accusations, blaming me for everything."

"What did he say?"

"He said *I* murdered Tiffany."

"What evidence did he have?"

"None whatsoever. He said it was a gut feeling. Can you believe it? I was in shock. After all these years together, I can't believe he'd accuse me of such a thing."

"What did you say?"

"I told him the same thing I told him the last time he asked. I had nothing to do with her death. I may not have liked the fact that he was having an affair, and I know it sounds strange, but I liked her."

If what she was telling me was true, I wondered what had provoked Tyler to confront her today.

Was he so lost in his grief, he needed someone to blame?

"What happened after he made the accusation?" I asked.

"I wanted to calm him down, so I suggested we have a seat and talk it through, like rational adults. Whenever he would get aggravated in the past, it almost always worked. Today, it just made him even madder. More yelling. More accusations. I didn't know what to do, so I asked him to leave."

"Considering he's dead, I'm guessing he didn't."

She shook her head. "What happened next ... well, I still can't believe it. He pulled a gun from beneath his shirt and started waving it around."

"What did he say?"

"More of the same. That *I* killed Tiffany. *I* took the one person who meant the most to him in life. *I* ripped her from him, and for that, *I* had to pay.

"What did you do?"

"The only thing I could think of doing. I took a step back, figuring if I could just get out of the room, I could get away. And then the gun went off. It took me a minute to realize I'd been hit in the leg. He shot me."

"But he's the one who's dead, so you must have found a way to defend yourself."

"After he shot me, I lunged at him, and he dropped the gun. We both dove for it, but I was closer. I grabbed it and aimed at him. 'Leave, and I won't shoot,' I said."

"What was his response?"

"He said he'd leave when I was dead. He came at me again, and I didn't want to do it, but I knew if he got the gun back, I wouldn't make it out alive. I closed my eyes, and I squeezed the trigger. I thought I'd just nick him, you know? Shoot him in a place that would slow him down, so I could get away. Then I ... I realized I shot him in the head."

Tears flooded down her face, and I reached out, placing my hand on her arm. The numbers on the bedside monitor began to rise, and then it started beeping. As I tried to calm her down, a nurse rushed in.

She glared at me and said, "She was fine a few minutes ago. What did you do?"

"I didn't *do* anything. We were just talking."

"Yeah, right. This visit's over. Get your things and get out."

32

I was back at Jana's house, updating Foley on the conversation I'd had with Jana at the hospital.

"What do you think?" he asked. "Do you believe her?"

"I don't know. I'm guessing Silas has been here. What did he have to say?"

"Not much. The time of death aligns with the timing of Jana's 911 call. We won't know much more until he does a full autopsy."

"Jana's wound was a through-and-through. Has the bullet been found?"

He nodded. "We ran the firearm's serial number through the registry. It's registered to Tyler."

If Tyler had intended on killing her, as Jana had suggested, what was his plan afterward? Turn himself in? Turn the gun on himself?

"Whitlock mentioned you visited with Landon Fairfax this morning," Foley said.

"The guy's a creep. When our conversation was over, and I turned to leave, he smacked me on the butt."

Foley pressed his fingers to his lips, a smirk tugging at them like he was struggling to hold back a laugh. "And you? What did you do?"

"I'm not sure you want to know."

"Is the guy still in one piece?"

For now.

"He's fine," I said.

"What did you talk about?"

"He admitted to confronting Tiffany, but he tried to play it down, like she'd exaggerated what he said to her. I disagree. She had no reason to lie."

"Sounds like we need to take a closer look at the guy."

"I'd love to take him down for Tiffany's murder, but so far, there's no evidence to suggest he did it. When Jana gave me the photos that were left on her car, I thought Landon had something to do with them. He didn't, though. Chad did."

Foley tilted his head to the side in that familiar way he always did before launching into lecture mode, and I had a good idea of what was coming next.

"Speaking of Chad, you've been keeping things from me," he said. "I'm not a fan of feeling like I'm the last one to find things out. When were you going to tell me?"

"Right after I spoke to Landon. Then I learned Tyler was dead, and we've been dealing with that ever since."

"When Silas mentioned it to me today, he seemed surprised to hear I didn't know anything about it."

"Yeah … sorry. I went to Chad's house last night."

Foley sighed. "And?"

"I asked him about the photos he left on Jana's car. He denied it at first, said it wasn't him. Then I told him we lifted a few prints, and one of them was his."

"What did he have to say for himself?"

"He hadn't admitted to taking the photos because he was afraid if he told the truth, we'd consider him a suspect."

"He'd be right. We do."

I huffed out a frustrated sigh. "Why don't people make it easier on themselves and tell the truth from the start?"

"These are strange times we live in. People seem a lot more on edge and nervous nowadays. It's almost like they're losing their faith in law enforcement, even though for the most part, we're still the good guys. And we are, of course, but for some, it needs to be proven to them."

Even so, it made me question Chad's innocence.

"I'll have Whitlock pay a visit to Landon and Chad, and we'll see what he thinks of the fellows," Foley said. "What do you have planned for the rest of the day?"

"This morning, I realized I've been going nonstop since the investigation began. When I don't take time to slow down, it's hard for me to see what's right in front of me. I think I'll go home and clear my head."

I planned to do just that until I turned and saw Jordan heading our way.

Foley stepped in front of me, hand outstretched as if to stop him. "How did you get in here?"

"I ... ahh, I walked in?"

Foley cupped a hand to the side of his mouth, yelling, "Higgins, get in here."

Moments later, Officer Higgins approached. He looked at Jordan, then Foley, and the color drained from his face. "Yeah?"

Foley thumbed in Jordan's direction. "You were supposed to be manning the front door."

"I needed to go to the bathroom. I was only gone for a minute."

"A minute is all it took for someone to waltz in here and contaminate my crime scene. Get him out of here."

"Sorry, boss," Higgins said.

"I don't need you to be sorry," Foley said. "I need you to do your job."

Jordan turned toward Foley. "Can't I just—"

"Not another word," Foley said, pointing toward the front door. "Out."

Higgins escorted Jordan to the door, and I followed. Once he was outside, I said, "Hey, Jordan. Can I talk to you for a minute?"

"Sure, and listen, I'm sorry about entering the house and causing a problem."

"It's fine. I'm assuming you know something about what happened here. How?"

Jordan tipped his head toward a white news van parked across the street. "They went live about twenty minutes ago. Lila was watching the news on her phone, and she came rushing into my office, saying reporters were talking about a possible homicide at Jana and Tyler's house."

Word traveled a little too fast for my liking sometimes.

In this tight-knit, loose-lipped town, it didn't shock me.

"What happened?" Jordan asked. "Do you know? Is Jana here?"

I considered how much I wanted to say.

"I think the less the public knows, the better, for now," I said.

"Come on, Detective. I'm not just anyone. I'm a friend."

I crossed my arms, thinking. "If I share some information with you, I need you to keep it to yourself for now. All right?"

"You got it."

"Tyler is dead, and Jana is in the hospital."

Jordan's mouth fell open, and he gasped. "I can't believe it. What happened?"

"She said he shot her in the leg."

I paused, assessing his demeanor as the news I'd just delivered set in.

His shock seemed genuine, his head shaking back and forth like he couldn't believe what he was hearing.

"Is she all right?" he asked.

"I just saw her. She's fine. I can tell you what Jana told me, but her story hasn't been verified yet. She said Tyler showed up at the house earlier today. He was angry, and he had a gun. He accused her of killing Tiffany, and he said she needed to pay for what she'd done. He shot her, she lunged at him, got control of the gun, and then killed him in self-defense."

"I don't even know what to say. I can't believe it."

"When's the last time you talked to Tyler?"

"Yesterday, in his office."

"How did he seem?"

"Detached, angry, and on edge. I tried talking to him. It was like he was there but wasn't, if you know what I mean, like I was talking through him not *to* him. I didn't think he'd been getting much sleep, and the way he smelled, it had been a while since he'd showered."

"Did he say anything to you about Jana?"

He mulled over the question. "I hate to say it, but he tried to convince me that Jana killed Tiffany."

"Did he have any proof to back up his claim?"

"He did not. I told him I disagreed with his accusation, and I tried to get him to calm down, which didn't work. He was too riled up."

"How did the conversation end?"

"He said a real friend would take him at his word. Ask me, he was trying to find someone to blame, and Jana was an easy target."

"Even if he'd decided to murder Jana, what was his

endgame?" I asked. "He knew he wouldn't get away with it. He used his own gun, for heaven's sake."

"Who knows? He's been irrational since Tiffany died. I mean, I knew he loved her, but I underestimated just how much. After our discussion, I was worried about him. I even swung by his house later that evening. He wasn't home. I called him, and he didn't answer. I figured he was still angry with me and needed some time to cool off. I wish I'd known what he was planning. If I had, maybe I could have talked him down. Maybe he'd still be alive."

"Have you been visited by one of Tiffany's neighbors since we spoke last?" I asked.

"I haven't, but I heard she talked to both Tyler and Jana. She thought one of them was involved in Tiffany's murder. Said something about having proof, a lighter or something with blood on it."

"How did they react to her accusation?"

"I don't know about Jana, but Tyler was upset. He told her to get lost."

"She's dead."

"Yeah, I heard. Hey, I'm going to take off, see if they'll let me see Jana."

I nodded.

It was time I went home and got everyone's story straight.

33

I was sitting on my balcony, patting Luka, as the investigation worked its way through my mind. I thought about everything I'd seen and everyone I talked to in the last week. It wasn't long before my thoughts turned to the lighter, and the fact Queenie may have been murdered because of it.

I picked my laptop up off the chair beside me and turned it on. Then I entered a description of the lighter and clicked to get the results. Turned out, there were thousands of black lacquer lighters with a chrome finish.

I tried again, this time by era, since the lighter had a vintage look to it. The '20s and '30s yielded similar results, but it wasn't until I searched the '40s that I saw something unexpected—the exact lighter Queenie found in Tiffany's kitchen.

As I sat there, staring at it, thoughts flooded my mind, connections being made faster than I could receive them.

Breathe.

Process.

Though I still had questions, it was all coming together.

I believed I knew who murdered Tiffany.

I just didn't know why.

34

I stepped into the real estate office and approached the front desk. Lila was dabbing her eyes with a tissue, which she then used to blow her nose.

"Hey, Lila," I said. "You doing okay?"

"I'm just ... you know, sad about Tyler," she said. "Can't believe he's dead. And Jana, I can't believe she shot him."

"We're still trying to figure it all out. Was Tyler at work yesterday?"

"Yeah, why?"

"Jordan said they had an argument in his office."

"I don't know anything about an argument. They were both talking about that crazy old woman, the one who says she's going to solve the murder."

"Queenie."

"Yeah, that's her."

"She talked to Tyler, right?"

"And Jordan. Accused them both of murder."

Yet Jordan had said he hadn't spoken to Queenie.

So many secrets.

So many lies.

It was time for them all to come out.

Lila grabbed another tissue from the box on her desk. "I'm sorry. I'm a blubbering mess."

"Don't be. It's understandable. Is Jordan here?"

"He's not. I can tell him you stopped by. Do you want to leave a message?"

"I'll just talk to him later. Listen, can I use your bathroom before I go?"

"Oh, yeah, sure. It's down the hall, third door on the left."

I thanked her, and as I headed down the hallway, a couple walked in the front door.

The timing couldn't have been better.

Jordan's office was also down the hall and to the left. I slipped inside and began looking around. His office looked a little different since my last visit. The framed photo of Audrey Hepburn was gone, replaced by another photo of a Labrador retriever. The box of candles was also gone.

I walked in front of his desk and sat in the chair, pulling the drawer open. There were a handful of file folders, several bottles of hand sanitizer, and at the bottom, a bottle of bourbon and a small box. I pulled the box out and opened it. A gun was inside. I moved to the next drawer. It contained hanging files, all arranged in alphabetical order.

"What are you doing in my office?"

I looked up to see Jordan standing in the doorway.

He wasn't pleased to see me.

"I came to talk to you," I said.

He stepped inside and closed the door, and I walked around the desk, sitting on in the chair on the opposite side.

He took a seat across from me. "Does talking to me involve snooping through my desk drawers?"

I shrugged. "I was bored."

And curious, among other things.

"Take a seat," I said.

"I have a meeting in twenty minutes."

"I'd cancel it if I were you."

"Why?"

I crossed one leg over the other. "It was you. *You* murdered Tiffany."

"I don't know why you're accusing me, but you're wrong."

"I'm not wrong, though. The first time we met, I saw a bottle of hand sanitizer in the cup on your desk, and there's even more in one of your desk drawers. I didn't think much of it, but now, I think you're a germaphobe. Ever since Queenie found the lighter in Tiffany's kitchen, something has been bothering me. I couldn't figure out why anyone would murder Tiffany and then take the time to go to the kitchen sink afterward, dropping the lighter in the process."

"What does any of this have to do with me?"

My newest theory was about to come to light.

"I imagine you wore gloves during the murder," I said. "At some point, some of Tiffany's blood must have gotten under your gloves, and you freaked out. You couldn't wait to get home to wash it off. No. You had to clean up then and there. That's when your lighter fell out of your pocket."

"Why would I own a lighter? I don't smoke."

"At first, I thought we were looking for a smoker. But lighters are used for a lot of things. And in your case, you used it to light the candles for your open houses. How am I doing so far?"

"You're not. I'm not going to sit here and listen to your false accusations."

"What happened to the Audrey Hepburn photo that was on your desk?"

His stiff, closed-off posture indicated his discomfort with my question.

"It fell off my desk by accident, and the glass broke," he said.

It sounded logical, but I didn't believe a word of it.

"I learned a few things today about the lighter found at Tiffany's house. It's part of a limited-edition collection, inspired by Audrey Hepburn."

"So?"

"It *is* your lighter, isn't it?"

"Just because I had a photo of Audrey Hepburn on my desk doesn't mean the lighter's mine, and it doesn't mean I use it to light candles. I use matches."

"Queenie wasn't lying when she talked to you yesterday, and she *did* talk to you, right after I saw her, I expect. When she told you about the blood on the lighter, as I imagine she did, you knew Tiffany's murder could be linked back to you. I'm guessing you followed Queenie to her house, and you killed her. Then you tore it apart, looking for the lighter, which *I* found under a piece of carpet in the guest room."

"I don't believe you."

"I don't care. A sample of your blood will prove it's yours, which proves you were in her house, and it will be enough to convict you of her murder. Your life is over."

He opened the top drawer of his desk, and I raised my gun, the one I'd been palming inside my bag. "If you're looking for your gun, you won't find it."

"You have it?"

"Sure do."

"Look, you don't need to point that thing at me."

"Don't I?"

"I wasn't going to pull a gun on you, if that's what you're thinking."

"Why did you open the drawer, then?"

He narrowed his eyes, staring at me for a time, like he was scheming, planning out his next move.

"Don't do it," I said.

"Don't do what?"

"Whatever you're planning."

"Or what?"

The second the words left his lips, he leapt over the desk, his hands reaching for my neck. But he was a few seconds too late. I had already fired.

35

I'd wanted nothing more than to shoot him dead when I fired my gun. I didn't just want justice for Tiffany. I wanted his life to end like he'd ended hers. But killing him would have been a far easier way for him to go than the life he'd have in prison, and I wanted him to live long enough to experience every excruciating moment of it.

I'd shot him in the shoulder, the impact just enough to stop him in his tracks. Lila rushed in, screaming when she realized what I'd done. I told her to call the police, and it wasn't long before they arrived, and Jordan was taken into custody.

After his gunshot wound was treated, Foley invited me to accompany them to the station where Jordan would be questioned. It was where we were now—Foley, Whitlock, and me, sitting in the interrogation room across from Jordan. We'd shown him the lighter and the smear of blood, which we were sure was his.

When it became clear to him that there was no way out, Jordan said, "You know something? I've been a disaster ever since this all started. It's strange to say, but I'm relieved it's over."

"You're *relieved*," I said. "Three people are dead, including one of my dearest friends. And for what?"

"I'm sorry."

"Save it. Sorry won't change anything. I want to know why you did it."

"Thinking back on the last week, it's all a blur."

"You better find clarity, because I want answers."

Foley gave me a look that indicated I should tone it down, but if I did what I wanted to do to Jordan, things would have been a lot worse.

"You can start by telling us why you killed Tiffany," Foley said.

Jordan went quiet for a time, and I waited.

Then he blurted out something I didn't expect.

"I'm having an affair with Jana," he said. "It's been going on for a while. One night, not long after Jana confronted Tiffany, I was over at Jana's house. We'd always been cautious when we met up, but we knew Tyler was out of town that night, and we didn't think much of it. As you know, Jana's house sits way back from the road, so we assumed no one would see us. We were in the living room, on the couch, kissing and stuff, and I look over, and there's Tiffany, outside, staring right at us through the window."

"What was she doing there?" I asked.

"She had a box of Tyler's things in her hands. She dropped the box and started running to her car. Jana went after her. Tiffany said she was there because she'd wanted to get Tyler's things out of her house. But she didn't want to see him, so she thought she could give it all to Jana. I think Tiffany also thought giving Jana the box was a way to assure her things were over with Tyler."

"Then what happened?"

"Jana asked Tiffany if she was going to tell Tyler what she

saw, and Tiffany said she wouldn't if Jana agreed to tell him herself. Problem is, Tyler had Jana sign a prenup when they got married."

"Why?"

"Tyler's grandfather was going to leave him a large sum of money when he died, and he didn't care much for Jana. His one condition was that Tyler get a prenup to protect himself, just in case."

"Let me guess," I said. "It included an infidelity clause."

"It did. If Tyler ever found out Jana was stepping out on him, she'd get nothing."

"So, Tiffany was murdered over money?" I asked.

"It was Jana's idea. I didn't want to do it. I swear."

"But you did."

"I regret it, now. Believe me."

"You regretted it so much, you killed again."

"You were right about me cleaning off in the sink after the murder. I didn't know there'd be so much blood, and when I saw it all over my skin, all I could think about was getting it off. I realized the next day I must have dropped the lighter in Tiffany's house, but I had no idea there was blood on it until I met Queenie."

"And Tyler? What's the real story there?"

Jordan shrugged and said, "I don't know. You'll have to talk to Jana."

But he did know.

And now I knew the story she'd told me was full of holes.

She'd put on a good show, an impressive one—tears, drama, the whole nine yards. I doubted any of it was real.

"Knowing how cunning Jana is, you should give some thought to what she's going to say when we talk to her," Foley said. "I think she'll turn on you. This might be your one shot at telling us the truth—all of it."

We all went quiet, letting his words sink in.

I hoped it had.

"How did it start, with Jana?" I asked.

"She hasn't been happy in the marriage in a long time," Jordan said. "It started out with her confiding in me, and I tried to help her to find ways to work things out. One night, after they got in a big fight, she showed up at my house. She started saying all these things about how different I am than Tyler. The next thing I know, she kisses me, and then we ... well, we took it from there."

"When did you find out about the prenup?"

"As soon as we started seeing each other on the regular. Tyler's grandfather was in the hospital at the time, and he wasn't expected to live much longer. She was going to file for divorce after his death, get her share of the money, and then, after it was all over, we were going to move from here and get a place together."

"But Tiffany spotted the two of you together."

"Jana lost her mind when she saw Tiffany," Jordan said. "I didn't view it as a bad thing, though. I figured all she'd lose was money that wasn't hers in the first place. She could still get a divorce, and we could be together. I thought I made enough for the both of us, but she was used to a certain kind of lifestyle, a much more expensive one than I can provide. She told me she loved me and wanted nothing more than to be with me, but I needed to take care of Tiffany, or it was over between us."

"How did you think you'd get away with it?" Foley asked.

"I would have, if it wasn't for that stupid lighter."

"No, you wouldn't have," I said.

"Jana thought if we gave you the photos that were left on her car, you'd assume they were left by the killer, and we'd look innocent, given no one knew we were dating."

"That's the thing about assumptions. They're not always

right. Earlier you told me you talked to Tyler yesterday. You said he was detached, angry, and on edge. Is any of that even true?"

He was quiet for a time, and then he said, "No, I'm sorry to say it's not. And as for Jana, I can't say whether she's being honest about what happened earlier today. I never thought she had it in her to kill him. I never would have agreed to it. She's not the woman I thought I knew, and I wish I'd never met her."

36

It was no surprise to learn the story Jana told me was fabricated. Once Silas analyzed the trajectory of the bullets, her version of events was torn to shreds. Silas believed Jana's gunshot wound was self-inflicted. She shot herself to make it seem like Tyler had gone there to kill her, and she'd acted in self-defense. I believed she invited Tyler over with every intention of killing him. If she could convince everyone that he was the bad guy and she was the victim, the entire inheritance would be hers.

I was standing at the local cemetery beside Ron Wheeler, admiring the headstone he'd chosen. In the center was a picture of Tiffany. She looked gorgeous, and so full of life. It was still hard to believe she was gone.

Ron held a bouquet of flowers in one hand, and with the

other, he took my hand and gave it a squeeze. "Thank you. I know that justice won't bring her back, but it's a start."

"I'd give just about anything to speak to her one last time."

"I think you can speak to her, and you should. Sure, you might not be able to see her, but I like to believe she'd still hear you somehow."

"I'd like to believe it, too."

"I talk to her here and there. Something will come to mind —a fond memory—and I just say what's on my mind. This may sound strange, but it's brought me a lot of comfort."

"It doesn't sound strange at all."

He released my hand and bent down, placing the roses in front of the headstone. Touching the stone, he said, "I sure do miss you, darling."

As he stood, he wiped a tear from his eye and said, "I think I'll leave you two to talk. Same time next week?"

"Same time. You let me know if you need anything between now and then, okay?"

"You betcha."

He waved and headed toward his car, leaving me alone with my thoughts. At first I struggled, trying to find my words.

And then ...

"I miss you. I miss your smile, your laugh, your advice. I wish you were here, and we were at the local pub, laughing over a couple of cocktails as we catch up on our crazy lives. It's not the same without you, and I doubt it will ever be. And even though I solved your case, it doesn't seem like it's enough. But I want you to know I'm looking out for your dad, just like you asked. Wherever you are, know I'm thinking of you and hoping you're at peace."

Message delivered, I stood there for a time, taking in the quiet stillness around me. As my eyes wandered, they came to land on a beautiful woman several rows away. She was walking hand in hand with a child. The more I stared at them, the more they reminded me of Tiffany and my daughter, Fallon, somehow.

The woman smiled, and I smiled back. Then I crouched down, placing the wildflowers I'd brought next to her father's roses. When I stood back up, I turned, looking for the woman and child. But they had disappeared.

It was like they'd never been there in the first place—*almost*.

The End

Thank you for reading Little Dark Deeds, book 12 in the Georgiana Germaine mystery series. I hope you enjoyed getting to know the characters in this story as much as I enjoyed writing them for you. You can find the series order (as of the date of this printing) in the "Books by Cheryl Bradshaw" section below.

...

In LITTLE SILENT STRANGER (Georgiana Germaine, Book 13)

Audrey Ashford thought it was just another walk through the woods

...

On the brink of leaving for college, she carries a secret she isn't ready to share, not even with her best friend. But as night falls and the shadows close in, Audrey realizes she's not alone. What begins as a familiar shortcut through the woods quickly turns into a deadly encounter, and by the time she reaches the ridge, it's too late.

Little Silent Stranger is a gripping mystery that pulls you into a world of secrets, betrayal, and the haunting question: how well do we ever really know the people around us?

...

Want a sneak peek? Here's an exclusive look at chapter one of LITTLE SILENT STRANGER

Audrey Ashford sat in front of her vanity mirror, applying a bit of color to her cheeks as she hummed along to Coldplay's "Speed of Sound" playing through the speakers of her stereo. Pleased with her overall look, she set the makeup brush to the side and stood, switching the music off. She walked to the window, her breath fogging the glass as she stared out at a dull, overcast sky. Grabbing her jacket out of the closet, she shut her bedroom door and headed downstairs.

She found her mother in the kitchen, chopping vegetables for the casserole she was making for a neighbor who'd just had a baby. A warm, savory fragrance of basil and garlic lingered in the air, and Audrey almost wished she wasn't leaving.

Her mother glanced up and said, "Are you headed over to Talia's house?"

"I am. We're finalizing plans for our college send-off party."

Her mother nodded, wiping her hands on a dish towel. "Are you driving over?"

"I've been in my room all day. I thought it would be good to get some fresh air, so I think I'll walk. Talia can bring me home when we're finished."

"Are you going along the street or cutting through the woods?"

"The woods."

"Be careful. It's gets dark fast at this time of year."

"I know. I will."

"When do you expect you'll be home?"

"Ten or eleven."

"Text me when you're on your way."

"Will do."

In a month's time, Audrey would be leaving for college. She wondered if her mother would still want her to check in.

Outside, the air was cool, settling around her like a soft

blanket. She cut through the side yard, heading toward the familiar path through the woods—a shortcut she'd taken hundreds of times. She loved taking this route, through the groves of trees, being one with nature.

Her foot crunched down on a smattering of dry leaves, a steady rhythm that almost always soothed her.

Tonight, though, the woods felt different—uneasy.

She pulled her jacket tighter around her. Somewhere in the silence, a twig snapped, and the hairs on the back of Audrey's neck pricked up.

"Hello?" Audrey called. "Is anyone there?"

There was no answer, just the steady rustle of the breeze.

She glanced around, seeing no one, convincing herself the noise was just a deer or a racoon, two of the forest's frequent visitors.

Audrey had been honest with her mother when she'd said she was going to Talia's to do some party planning, but that wasn't the only reason. There was a secret she'd been carrying, heavy and suffocating, the weight of it pressing on her with every step. As she thought about seeing Talia, the person she trusted most, she wasn't sure she was ready to share it yet. She wondered if the moment would ever feel right or what would happen once her truth was revealed.

A faint crack echoed nearby, much too deliberate to be just a branch snapping under the weight of an animal, and she froze, heart pounding. Another rustle came from deeper in the shadows, and Audrey's eyes darted through the trees. She realized she wasn't alone. Something—or—someone was there, hidden but watching.

Audrey started moving again, quickening her steps until she was almost at a swift jog.

One more minute, and Talia's house would come into view, rising over the ridge.

Two more minutes, and she'd be safe ...

A figure stepped out of from behind a tree, a little silent stranger grabbing her from behind, hot breath pressing against the back of her neck.

Before she could scream, a hand clamped over her mouth, another pressing something sharp against her side.

Then everything faded to black.

...

Order your copy of Little Silent Stranger today at CherylBradshawStore.Com (and a big thank you to all those who order direct from the store—it is appreciated), or you can order on your preferred retailer.

ENJOY LITTLE DARK DEEDS?

You can show your appreciation by leaving a review on Amazon, Barnes & Noble, Apple Books, Google Play, Kobo, or Goodreads.

If you write a review, please be sure to email Cheryl (cheryl@authorcherylbradshaw(dot)com) so she can express her gratitude. She does her best to reply to as many emails as she can, and she appreciates every piece of mail she receives.

ABOUT CHERYL BRADSHAW

Cheryl Bradshaw is a New York Times and 11-time USA Today bestselling author writing in multiple genres, including mystery, thriller, romantic suspense, supernatural suspense, and poetry. She is a Shamus Award finalist for best private eye novel of the year, an eFestival of Words winner for best thriller, and has published over fifty books since 2011.

When she's not writing, Cheryl loves jet-setting to new countries, playing with her grandkids, high tea, and pursuing a wishful side career as a professional food tester of wine and cheese.

NEVER MISS ONE OF CHERYL'S BOOK'S AGAIN!

Sign up for Cheryl Bradshaw's "Killer Newsletter" today to be the first to know when a new book is released and to enter to win fun bookish swag. You'll also receive some fantastic book freebies just for joining!

Learn more by visiting CherylBradshawStore.Com and adding your email address on the SIGN UP AND SAVE form at the bottom of the home page. Your email in for our eyes only and will not be shared with anyone else.

BOOKS BY CHERYL BRADSHAW

Sloane Monroe Series

Silent as the Grave (Prequel, Book 0)

When the body of Rebecca Barlow is found floating in the lake, private investigator Sloane Monroe takes on her very first homicide.

Black Diamond Death (Book 1)

Charlotte Halliwell has a secret. But before revealing it to her sister, she's found dead.

Murder in Mind (Book 2)

A woman is found murdered, the serial killer's trademark "S" carved into her wrist.

I Have a Secret (Book 3)

Doug Ward has been running from his past for twenty years. But after his fourth whisky of the night, he doesn't want to keep quiet, not anymore.

Stranger in Town (Book 4)

A frantic mother runs down the aisles, searching for her missing daughter. But little Olivia is already gone.

Bed of Bones (Book 5) (USA Today Bestselling Book)

Sometimes even the deepest, darkest secrets find their way to the surface.

Flirting with Danger (Book 5.5) A Sloane Monroe Short Story

A fancy hotel. A weekend getaway. For Sloane Monroe, rest has finally arrived, until the lights go out, a woman screams, and Sloane's nightmare begins.

Hush Now Baby (Book 6) (USA Today Bestselling Book)

Serena Westwood tiptoes to her baby's crib and looks inside, startled to find her newborn son is gone.

Dead of Night (Book 6.5) A Sloane Monroe Short Story

After her mother-in-law is fatally stabbed, Wren is seen fleeing with the bloody knife. Is Wren the killer, or is a dark, scandalous family secret to blame?

Gone Daddy Gone (Book 7) (USA Today Bestselling Book)

A man lurks behind Shelby in the park. Who is he? And why does he have a gun?

Smoke & Mirrors (Book 8) (USA Today Bestselling Book)

Grace Ashby wakes to the sound of a horrifying scream. She races down the hallway, finding her mother's lifeless body on the floor in a pool of blood. Her mother's boyfriend Hugh is hunched over her, but is Hugh really her mother's killer?

...

Sloane Monroe Stories: Deadly Sins

...

Deadly Sins: Sloth (Book 1)

Darryl has been shot, and a mysterious woman is sprawled out on the floor in his hallway. She's dead too. Who is she? And why have they both been murdered?

Deadly Sins: Wrath (Book 2)

Headlights flash through Maddie's car's back windshield, someone following close behind. When her car careens into a nearby tree, the chase comes to an end. But for Maddie, the end is just the beginning.

Deadly Sins: Lust (Book 3)

Marissa Calhoun sits alone on a beach-like swimming hole nestled on Australia's foreshore. Tonight, the lagoon is hers and hers alone. Or is it?

Deadly Sins: Greed (Book 4)

It was just another day for mob boss Giovanni Luciana until he took his car for a drive.

Deadly Sins: Envy (Book 5)

A cryptic message. A missing niece. And only twenty-four hours to pay.

Deadly Sins: Pride (Book 6)

A secret lies within the Kingston mansion's walls, a secret that's about to bring the past into the present.

...

Sloane & Maddie, Peril Awaits (Co-Authored with Janet Fix)

...

The Silent Boy (Book 1)

In the hallway of a local tavern, six-year-old Louie Alvarez waits for his mother to take him home. A scream rips through the air, followed by the sound of a gun being fired. Louie freezes, then turns, with a single thought on his mind: RUN.

The Shadow Children (Book 2)

Within the tunnels of the historic port city of Savannah, fourteen-year-old Andi Leland has her mind set on freedom—not just for herself but for all the other teens who have come before her.

The Broken Soul (Book 3)

When the party of a lifetime becomes a party to the death, the lines become blurred. Friends become enemies. Drugs become weapons. And that's just the beginning.

The Widow Maker (Book 4)

A friend murdered. A business in trouble. A marriage struggling to survive. And that's just the beginning.

The Familiar Stranger (Book 5)

As semi-retired private detective Sloane Monroe unwinds at a luxurious spa retreat in North Carolina, a jarring phone call shatters her peaceful getaway.

...

Georgiana Germaine Series

...

Little Girl Lost (Book 1)

For the past two years, former detective Georgiana "Gigi" Germaine has been living off the grid, until today, when she hears some disturbing news that shakes her.

Little Lost Secrets (Book 2)

When bones are discovered inside the walls during a home renovation, Georgiana uncovers a secret that's linked to her father's untimely death thirty years earlier.

Little Broken Things (Book 3)

Twenty-year-old Olivia Spencer sits at her desk in her mother's bookshop, dreaming about her upcoming wedding. The store may be closed, but she's not alone, and her dream is about to become her worst nightmare.

Little White Lies (Book 4)

When a serial killer sweeps through the streets of Cambria, California, Georgiana Germaine gets swept up into a tangled web of deception and lies.

Little Tangled Webs (Book 5)

What if you knew the person you loved was murdered, but no one else believed you? Eighteen-year-old Harper Ellis knows she's right, and she's prepared to risk her life to prove it.

Little Shattered Dreams (Book 6)

At fifty-five, Quinn Abernathy has been through her fair share of experiences in life. And tonight, her past is coming back to haunt her.

Little Last Words (Book 7)

After living in a verbally abusive relationship for the past six years, twenty-seven-year-old Penelope Barlow has finally found the courage to leave. But can she escape ... with her life?

Little Buried Secrets (Book 8)

In a split-second, a car collides with Margot, and she finds herself hurdling through the air, her bike going one way as she goes the other. Her mind whirls in this moment, as she thinks about her life and just how much she doesn't want to die.

Little Stolen Memories (Book 9)

In a secluded cabin deep within the woods, an ominous stranger is about to change the lives of six unsuspecting teenagers forever.

Little Empty Promises (Book 10)

As librarian Cordelia Bennett prepares to lock up for the night, a mysterious sound startles her. She turns. The fading light reveals a chilling presence in the shadows, and Cordelia realizes she's not alone.

Little Hidden Fears (Book 11)

Noelle Winters has just thrown the perfect engagement party ... or so she believes. As the evening winds down and the toast is about the commence, the lights go out. And for someone, the night has just turned deadly.

Little Dark Deeds (Book 12)

It's Georgiana Germaine's wedding day. But when one of her closest friends is noticeably absent from the ceremony, Georgiana worries something sinister is to blame.

Little Silent Stranger (Book 13)

Walking the wooded path to her friend's house, Audrey Ashford soon realizes she's not alone. What begins as a familiar shortcut quickly turns into a deadly encounter, and by the time she reaches the ridge, it's far too late.

...

Addison Lockhart Series

...

Grayson Manor Haunting (Book 1)

When Addison Lockhart inherits Grayson Manor after her mother's untimely death, she unlocks a secret that's been kept hidden for over fifty years.

Rosecliff Manor Haunting (Book 2)

Addison Lockhart jolts awake. The dream had seemed so real. Eleven-year-old twins Vivian and Grace were so full of life, but they couldn't be. They've been dead for over forty years.

Blackthorn Manor Haunting (Book 3)

Addison Lockhart leans over the manor's window, gasping when she feels a hand on her back. She grabs the windowsill to brace herself, but it's too late-- she's already falling.

Belle Manor Haunting (Book 4)

A vehicle barrels through the stop sign, slamming into the car Addison Lockhart is inside before fleeing the scene. Who is the driver of the other car? And what secrets within the walls of Belle Manor will provide the answer?

Crawley Manor Haunting (Book 5)

Something evil is coming. Something dark. Something seeking to destroy everything and everyone in its path. And Addison Lockhart is the only one who can stop it.

...

Till Death do us Part Novella Series

...

Whispers of Murder (Book 1)

It was Isabelle Donnelly's wedding day, a moment in time that should have been the happiest in her life...until it ended in murder.

Echoes of Murder (Book 2)

When two women are found dead at the same wedding, medical examiner Reagan Davenport will stop at nothing to discover the identity of the killer.

...

Stand-Alone Novels

...

Eye for Revenge (USA Today Bestselling Book)

Quinn Montgomery wakes to find herself in the hospital. Her childhood best friend Evie is dead, and Evie's four-year-old son witnessed it all. Traumatized over what he saw, he hasn't spoken.

The Perfect Lie

When true-crime writer Alexandria Weston is found murdered on the last stop of her book tour, fellow writer Joss Jax steps in to investigate.

<u>Hickory Dickory Dead</u> (USA Today Bestselling Book)

Maisie Fezziwig wakes to a harrowing scream outside. Curious, she walks outside to investigate, and Maisie stumbles on a grisly murder that will change her life forever.

<u>Roadkill</u> (USA Today Bestselling Book)

Suburban housewife Juliette Granger has been living a secret life ... a life that's about to turn deadly for everyone she loves.